"Why can't Aunt Sophie stay with us?"

Sophie quickly stifled the smile teasing her lips. Out of the mouths of babes. "That's a great idea. I'd love to take care of you while your uncle is on duty."

"Cool." She turned and ran from the room, shouting, "Linney, Aunt Sophie is going to stay with us."

Zach was glaring. "You had no right to override me."

"I didn't. It was Katie's idea. Besides, you know it's the best solution. I'm here, I'm available and the kids want me to stay. What do you have against me, Zach?"

He fisted his hands on the counter, inhaling slowly. "You mean because you show up here out of the blue and assume you can just become part of our lives? I'm not comfortable leaving my kids with a stranger."

"A nanny would be a stranger. What's the difference?" He had no answer to that. She couldn't blame him for being protective of the children. "I want to do this, Zach. I won't let anything happen to them."

Lorraine Beatty was raised in Columbus, Ohio, but now calls Mississippi home. She and her husband, Joe, have two sons and five grandchildren. Lorraine started writing in junior high and is a member of RWA and ACFW, and a charter member and past president of Magnolia State Romance Writers. In her spare time she likes to work in her garden, travel and spend time with her family.

Books by Lorraine Beatty

Love Inspired

The Orphans' Blessing

Mississippi Hearts

Her Fresh Start Family
Their Family Legacy
Their Family Blessing

Home to Dover

Protecting the Widow's Heart
His Small-Town Family
Bachelor to the Rescue
Her Christmas Hero
The Nanny's Secret Child
A Mom for Christmas
The Lawman's Secret Son
Her Handyman Hero

Visit the Author Profile page at Harlequin.com for more titles.

The Orphans' Blessing

Lorraine Beatty

LOVE INSPIRED

INSPIRATIONAL ROMANCE

LOVE INSPIRED®
INSPIRATIONAL ROMANCE

PLEASE RECYCLE
THIS PRODUCT IS RECYCLABLE

Recycling programs
for this product may
not exist in your area.

ISBN-13: 978-1-335-48833-6

The Orphans' Blessing

This edition published by arrangement with Harlequin Books S.A.

For questions and comments about the quality of this book, please contact us at CustomerService@Harlequin.com.

Love Inspired
22 Adelaide St. West, 40th Floor
Toronto, Ontario M5H 4E3, Canada
www.Harlequin.com

Printed in U.S.A.

And forgive us our debts,
as we forgive our debtors.
—*Matthew* 6:12

To my two new great-grandsons—
Kai and Forrest,
you have blessed our lives beyond belief.

Chapter One

Sophie Armstrong pulled to a stop in front of the charming old home on the tree-lined street in the small town of Blessing, Mississippi. Her heart pounded fiercely inside her chest as she admired the pale blue two-story house with a wraparound porch nestled behind a white picket fence. It was a storybook house. Exactly the kind of home she would have expected her sister, Madeline, to live in.

Only she didn't live here anymore. She and her husband had been killed in a car accident five months ago, leaving behind three children. Her nieces and nephew. Her family. All the family she had left in the world.

She felt a tightness in her chest. If only she'd been able to track her sister down sooner, they could have reconciled. Madeline could have told her why she'd disappeared fifteen years ago, leaving a hole in Sophie's life that had never been filled. She'd come down here from Ohio to find her sister's children in hopes that the emptiness could finally be filled.

The chime of her cell jolted her out of her thoughts.

She smiled at the name appearing on her phone. Angela Crawford. Her best friend and manager of Billie's Boutique Gifts, the shop Sophie's aunt, Billie Armstrong, had owned and she'd inherited after her death. Sophie had left the business in Angela's capable hands when she came to Mississippi.

"Are you there yet?" Angela asked.

"I just pulled up." Sophie's gaze landed on the giant live oak with a swing hanging from one thick branch.

"Don't worry. It'll all turn out fine. I have faith."

"So do I, but that doesn't mean it'll turn out the way I want." She inhaled a ragged breath.

"I know this last year hasn't been easy for you."

Sophie huffed. "You mean because it reads like a script from a bad soap opera? Only living relative passes away, fiancé walks out, I find out my long-lost sister is dead, and surgery makes it impossible for me to have children."

"I know, but you need to think of those events as blessings."

Sophie sighed inwardly. She loved Angela dearly, but sometimes her optimistic outlook grew tiresome.

"First, if you hadn't run into that old friend of your sister's, you wouldn't have known where to start searching for her. Then your aunt Billie passed away, leaving you a nice inheritance that made it possible for you to hire a private investigator to look for Madeline. As for that fiancé of yours, Greg, good riddance to him. Your surgery was heartbreaking but you found your nieces and nephew. They can be the children you won't have."

Hearing her list of losses spoken aloud stung. "Except, they have an uncle who's their guardian now. I can't walk in and just claim them."

"No, but you said he's a single guy and a pilot to boot, so he may be looking for some way out."

"I wouldn't be."

Angela sighed. "Okay. I know when I'm talking to a wall. Give me a call after you've met them. I want to hear all about it."

Sophie agreed, then ended the call and gathered her courage. Time to meet her sister's children.

The air was sweet with the scent of newly mown grass as she made her way up onto the broad front porch, noticing the swing at one end and the cozy rockers at the other. Toys, balls and water guns were scattered across the planks. Evidence of the children who lived here.

She stared at the front door. On the other side were her nieces and nephew. Would they look like Madeline? Or did they take after their father? Closing her eyes, she prayed that finding her sister's family would finally erase the sense of abandonment she'd felt for so long.

The door opened and a little girl looked up at her with wide blue eyes exactly like Madeline's. This must be the youngest child, Linney, which was a nickname for Madeline. Sophie smiled and bent forward. "Hello. I'm…"

The little girl's eyes widened. She took a step backward, then ran off, calling for her uncle.

Stunned, Sophie stood frozen. She hadn't meant to scare the child. She peered inside the house to see a tall dark-haired man striding toward her. His brown eyes widened and she saw him brace in surprise. The little girl peeked around the corner at the end of the foyer. He stopped in front of her, a deep scowl on his angular face.

"Can I help you?"

His tone held an odd combination of surprise and caution. She realized how imposing he was with his broad shoulders and muscular arms. Her throat tightened and she tried to swallow and speak at the same time, but only succeeded in making herself cough.

She took a deep breath and forced a smile. "I'm Sophie Armstrong. Madeline's younger sister. I've been searching for her and… I… Uh…"

The man's jaw flexed rapidly and his eyes darkened to black. "Madeline had no family."

Sophie struggled to process what he was saying. "What? No. That's not true. She had me. Our parents are gone but I'm here." She rubbed her cheek, trying to make sense of it all. "Why would Madeline say she had no family?"

"I wouldn't know. But she never mentioned a sister or anyone else."

A boy about thirteen moved into the foyer. He took one look at her, frowned, then walked away. This was certainly not how she envisioned her first meeting with her sister's family.

The man scanned her up and down as if assessing her validity. "Madeline and my brother Dean were killed in a car accident."

"Yes, I know."

"Uncle Zach, who's at the door?" A girl around ten years old entered the foyer, and like the other two children, her eyes widened when she saw Sophie. Then she burst into tears.

Sophie's heart twisted inside her chest. She'd made

a mess of things. She should have called ahead. "I'm so sorry. I never meant to upset anyone. I just—"

The uncle turned and spoke softly to the girl, then faced her again. "What did you expect? You look just like their mother."

Sophie hadn't considered the effect her sudden appearance might have on her nieces and nephew. All she'd thought about was finding her family. Her resemblance to her sister was mentioned frequently when they were young. She'd never anticipated it would still be a factor after all these years.

"What do you want?"

She swallowed the lump of fear in her throat his deep voice had triggered. "I want to see my sister's children. They're my only family now."

He stiffened, squaring his shoulders like a soldier called to action. "They are *my* family. I'm their legal guardian."

Heat shot up her neck and she lowered her gaze. "Yes, of course. But I'm their mother's sister, which makes you and I related, sort of. If we could talk for a few minutes, I'm sure I can explain everything."

The uncle gripped the door handle and for a brief moment she feared he'd shut it in her face.

"Not right now. I need to do some damage control. You'll have to come back later."

She was disappointed but not surprised. "When?" She wasn't going to be turned away for good. This was too important.

"I don't know. Tomorrow maybe. I'll have to see how the children are."

Normally a very compliant woman, the sudden rise

of fierce determination inside took her by surprise, but she couldn't ignore it. "I want to meet my nieces and nephew. I have questions and I'm not leaving Blessing until I have answers."

The man's eyes narrowed. She held her breath. Had she gone too far? He shifted his weight, then finally spoke.

"Where are you staying?"

"The Azalea Inn."

"I'll call you there and set up a meeting." He started to close the door.

"Wait." She dug a scrap of paper from her purse and scribbled her phone number. "Call my cell phone. I don't want to miss your call. And I should have your number, as well."

He took the paper, scribbled his number at the bottom and tore it off. He handed it to her, glared then closed the door, leaving her with a hot, aching sensation in her chest. She'd botched things terribly. Angela had suggested repeatedly that Sophie call ahead and make arrangements to meet Madeline's children, but Sophie had been afraid the uncle, Zach Conrad, would refuse. She'd decided to be more like Madeline and confront the situation directly.

Maddie had always been the brave one, unafraid of anything. She'd been the one others envied and emulated. She'd been tall, beautiful and outgoing, the one with all the energy and spunk, the very things that kept her at odds with their mother. Sophie, on the other hand, was shorter, the introvert who tried to keep the peace and fade into the background as much as possible.

Well, she wasn't going to fade anywhere this time.

She'd taken time off from managing her aunt's gift shop in Gahanna, Ohio, a suburb of Columbus, to come to Blessing, and she meant what she'd told Zach. She wasn't leaving until she met her family.

Sliding behind the wheel of her car, she started back to the inn. At least she'd caught a glimpse of her sister's children. Linney, the little one, looked like her mother, with her blue eyes and light blond hair. The boy, DJ, named after his father Dean Joseph, had dark brown eyes and hair like his uncle. Katie, the middle one, had pretty brown eyes and light brown hair and her mom's big smile.

Those glimpses would have to hold her until she could sit down with them face to face. And she planned on pestering Zach until he gave in.

But what if he didn't?

Zach closed the front door and offered up a fervent prayer for strength. The children were likely traumatized by the sudden appearance of their aunt. He certainly was. He would have challenged the woman's claim but there was no doubt she was related to Madeline. The family resemblance was too strong. The question now was how to deal with her?

"DJ, Katie, Linney. Family meeting pronto." He waited for them to assemble in the family room, trying to gauge their emotional state. Who was he kidding? He had no idea how to read the kids. "We need to talk about what just happened."

Talk. The last thing he wanted to do. He avoided talking at all costs. He'd found it only complicated things, but this time he couldn't behave as if nothing had happened.

Linney spoke up first, her eyes puzzled. "Who was that lady? She looked like Mommy. Why did she look like Mommy?"

Zach moved to sit beside her on the sofa, slipping an arm around her as he searched for the words to explain to a six-year-old. "She's your mom's sister."

Katie looked up from her position on the floor; her eyes were still moist. She stroked the head of the family dog, Lumpy, a brown Lab who lay beside her. "Linney is my sister but we don't look alike."

DJ emitted a loud grunt. "But Dad and Uncle Zach did, goofus."

Zach shot him a warning glare.

"Is she coming back?" Katie sat up, her forehead creased in a deep frown, her long light brown hair falling over her shoulders.

"Do you want her to?" He scanned the three children, assessing their reactions. They appeared more surprised than traumatized.

DJ shrugged. "Whatever." He slid the headphones from around his neck onto his ears.

Katie nodded. "She could tell us about Mommy when she was a kid."

Linney, her head still resting against his shoulder, looked up at him with big blue eyes filled with confusion. "Maybe she likes baking cookies like Mommy did."

Zach stifled a sigh. He'd hoped the kids would want no part of the new relative, but he should have known better. He'd have to deal with this and try to protect the kids as much as possible. The woman had said she had questions. Well, he had a few dozen of his own.

"All right. I'll have her come over again and you can talk to her."

Katie smiled. "When?"

"Soon."

After the children drifted off to their rooms, Zach called his friend Hank Blair. Hank owned a local flight charter service, Southland Charters, where Zach occasionally worked during his weeks off from his job as an oil rig chopper pilot. He needed some perspective on this. He was too emotionally involved to think clearly, and he was already questioning his decision to invite the sister back to the house.

"Hey, buddy. What has you calling at this time of day?"

Zach wasted no time on pleasantries. "Maddie had a sister."

"What? I thought she was an orphan or something."

"That's what she always claimed, but apparently she had a younger sister who is very much alive and who came knocking on my door."

"Are you sure she's the sister? I mean, maybe it's a scam or something."

Zach rubbed his forehead, then sank onto a stool at the kitchen counter, "No, she's the spitting image of Maddie. No question, though she's shorter and not as vibrant as Maddie was."

"Why do you suppose Maddie lied?"

"I don't know. But this woman showed up here out of the blue looking like the kids' mom and scared them half to death."

"Are they okay?"

"I guess. I'm not good at reading them, but they want her to come back so they can meet her."

"Is that a good idea?"

Zach tapped the counter with his fingers. "I don't know, but I can't ignore her. Besides, I have a lot of questions, mainly why she chose to show up now. This isn't a good time for the kids. They were just getting their feet under them and now they have to deal with a long lost relative who's a replica of their mother."

"You think she has some ulterior motive?"

Zach hadn't considered that. "Like what? It's not like there's a huge inheritance to lay claim to."

"But there are three children."

An icy chill raced through Zach's veins. "You think she might want custody?" He would not let that happen. "I'm the legal guardian. Nothing she can do about that."

"Unless she proves you're unfit."

Could she? He certainly had no experience being a dad to three kids. Half the time he was making things up as he went. His biggest fear was that he'd fail the children and not be the kind of parent his brother and sister-in-law had been. Dean had always been the domestic one. He'd followed in their father's footsteps as a contractor, and he loved being a dad and a husband. He was content with the family life.

Zach had never been content anywhere. As long as he could remember, he'd longed for adventure, mainly in the skies. He'd wanted to be a pilot from the time he'd first seen an airplane at a local air show.

"Hey, forget what I just said," Hank said. "You're a good dad to those kids. They love you."

Zach shook his head. "I don't know. I'm living each day on a wing and a prayer."

"Just like the rest of us, pal. Don't be so hard on yourself. And don't anticipate trouble before it arrives. My advice? Let her meet the kids and see what happens from there. Just remember, she's their aunt. Other than you, she's their only family. Maybe it'll be good to have her around to talk about their mom."

Zach grunted a tacit agreement, then ended the call. Talking. The one thing he was lousy at. The kids' pediatrician had recommended they meet with a psychologist to help deal with their grief. He'd told Zach when the children were ready to talk about their parents, they would. Zach had taken that as a signal to stand back and wait. Maybe that hadn't been the right approach.

At any rate he had to deal with this sister thing. Maybe, after she met the kids, she'd go back home and he could return to focusing on their daily routine. He pulled the scrap of paper with her phone number on it from his pocket. The sooner he got this over with, the sooner Aunt Sophie would be out of their lives.

The anxiety in Sophie's chest swirled relentlessly. She knew she needed more than the restful quiet of her cozy room at the historic inn to restore her peace. Turning toward the outskirts of town, she drove out to the landmark sign designating the location of the Blessing Bridge and parked nearby.

Tabitha Fleming, the owner of the Azalea Inn had told her about the bridge and its intriguing history.

"Back in the fifties, a woman whose son had polio came to the bridge and prayed for healing. Three weeks later her son started to improve. Three weeks after that he was cured. Since then, people started coming to the bridge and reporting amazing answers to their prayers. Everyone comes away with a different experience, but no one comes away empty. The blessings aren't instantaneous but they always come, usually in a form we aren't expecting."

A small plaque marked the entrance to a narrow path into the woods.

The Blessing Bridge. A place of hope and peace.
Lift your cares to the Lord with a sincere heart
and a humble spirit and return renewed.

The wooded area was quiet and isolated. She'd expected a well-known landmark to be in the middle of a park, but the path wound between the trees beneath the dappled sunlight. The bridge arched above a large pond, its banks choked with vegetation.

In the distance, barely visible between the trees, were the ruins of the Afton Grove Plantation. She'd learned the land here belonged to the descendants of the family who had generously granted public access to the bridge. With a little imagination, she could see how the property might have looked years ago with manicured gardens and neatly trimmed shrubs and flowers planted in colorful splashes along a sloping lawn to the water's edge.

Her hand trailed along the bridge railing, admiring the graceful design. A thick vine curled along the top edge of the railing, its large green leaves a pleasant contrast to the weathered wood. It reminded her of the

Bible verse "I am the vine, you are the branches." She was a branch of Maddie's family vine.

Stopping in the middle of the bridge, she stared at the water. It was peaceful here despite the unkempt grounds. Closing her eyes, she took a deep breath and allowed her thoughts to turn upward. She didn't know how long she prayed, but when she opened her eyes, she felt grounded, safe and secure. She hadn't heard any whispered words from the Lord or been filled with life-changing emotions, but the fatigue and worry she'd carried with her onto the bridge were gone and that was enough.

Slowly, she made her way back down the path. Her phone rang as she stepped into the parking area. Zach Conrad's name appeared on the screen. A warm rush coursed through her veins. She pushed Accept with a shaky finger.

"Miss Armstrong. This is Zach Conrad."

"I've been looking forward to your call."

"Right." He sounded irritated. "Well, why don't you come by the house tomorrow around one? The kids have asked to see you."

She kept herself from shouting with joy. "Thank you so much, Mr. Conrad. I'll be there." She ended the call and clutched the cell phone to her chest. He'd agreed to let her see the children and they were anxious to meet her.

But what if they didn't like her? What if—

She shut down the rush of negative thoughts. Angela was right; she had to be more positive. She glanced back at the wooded path. Her prayers had definitely been answered.

* * *

Zach bowed his head for the benediction. As usual, Pastor Miller's sermon had hit home, reminding him that God was in control of his life and not Zach. It was something he struggled with on a daily basis. He would turn his life over to the Lord in the morning and a half hour later he was taking it back into his own hands, trying to fix whatever popped up.

Stepping into the aisle, he waited for the kids to file out of the pew. He glanced up and caught sight of Sophie Armstrong at the back of the sanctuary. His conscience pricked like a blackberry branch. He should have invited her to join them this morning. It would have been the decent thing to do, but he'd been too shocked and surprised by her appearance to think clearly.

As he watched, Mrs. Hovak and her mother stopped to speak to Sophie. Not good. The ladies weren't known for their tact. The news of a surprise sister would start tongues wagging in a small town like Blessing. The smile on Sophie's face quickly faded into one of discomfort. When she took a step backward, Zach knew it was time to act.

"Kids, wait for me outside. I need to talk to someone."

Zach quickly wound his way past the other church members, then gently took Sophie's elbow and smiled broadly. "There you are. The family is waiting." The look of gratitude in her hazel eyes emboldened him. "Sorry to take her away, ladies, but we need to be going."

Sophie walked close to his side as they headed toward the door. "Thank you."

Her voice was breathless and he could feel her shaking. "Let me guess. They were bombarding you with questions about Madeline."

She nodded. "I didn't know how to answer them. I don't even have the answers myself."

He reached for the door handle at the same time she did and his hand landed on top of her smaller one. It was cool and clammy. A wave of sympathy washed through him.

Safely outside the church, she stopped and pulled her keys from her purse. "Thank you for coming to my rescue. I didn't know how I was going to get away from them."

"They mean well. They're just curious. The fact that you look so much like Madeline only makes it worse."

She pressed her lips together and brushed a stray hair from her forehead. "I'll be better prepared next time."

He couldn't let her worry over this. "Why don't you come to the house now? You can visit with the kids while I get the food ready for the grill."

Her hazel eyes lit up. "Are you sure? I would love that."

Her smile washed through him like a warm summer breeze. "Good. We'll see you in a few minutes." He held her gaze a moment, captivated by the blue flecks in her hazel eyes. He cleared his throat and smiled. "See you later then."

He watched her walk away, suddenly aware of how small and fragile she was, not at all like her older sister. His mind filled with questions. Probably the same ones the women had been asking. He'd have his answers soon enough.

He hoped.

* * *

Sophie's emotions were on a roller coaster as she drove to the Conrad house. She'd enjoyed the church service, even though it was different from the one she attended back home. The message had touched her. The verses had been encouraging and reminded her that all things worked for good if she had faith. She hoped that meant this afternoon's meeting would go smoothly. The people she'd met were all very nice until the two women cornered her at the back of the sanctuary.

The last person she'd expected to come to her rescue was Zach Conrad. His sudden appearance had been a godsend. He'd skillfully whisked her away and out of the church with a kindness and consideration that had surprised her. His cool reception yesterday had troubled her, but his invitation to come to the house now had eased much of that.

Sophie stood at the front door of the Conrad house a short while later, her heart racing again, but this time from eager anticipation instead of fear. She'd spent a restless night trying to envision how the first meeting with her nieces and nephew would play out. She knew better than to indulge in such fantasizing. Life never unfolded the way she expected. She'd decided to let that all go and simply take it one step at a time.

The door opened. Zach stood there, tall, dark but without the defensiveness from yesterday. He grinned and gestured her inside. "Come in. The kids are looking forward to talking to you. They have a lot of questions. So do I."

She couldn't miss the warning behind his easy tone.

She met his gaze and refused to flinch. "Me, too." She followed him into the living room.

"Aunt Sophie is here."

Zach's shout brought instant results. DJ emerged from the kitchen, the girls pounded down the stairs squealing. A large brown dog lumbered behind them. The youngest reached her first.

"Hello, Linney," Sophie greeted her.

"How did you know my name? Did my mommy tell you?"

Sophie's heart pinched. "No. A friend told me." No need to explain about the private investigator.

Katie approached more slowly. "You look like my mom. It's kinda weird."

Sophie reached down and stroked the dog's soft fur. "I'm sure it is, but we always looked alike. Except your mom was…"

DJ dropped into one of the chairs. "Mom was taller and prettier." The belligerent tone in his voice brought a stern reprimand from his uncle.

Sophie quickly dismissed his hurtful words. "Yes, she was."

Katie smiled and stroked the dog. "This is Lumpy. Mommy called him that 'cause he just lays around like a brown lump most of the time."

The dog lifted his head, sniffed Sophie's hand, then nuzzled his nose into her palm, making her chuckle. "Hello there, Lumpy."

Linney stepped closer. "He likes you."

"I like him, too."

Zach gently touched Linney's head. "I'll leave y'all to get acquainted while I get the burgers ready."

DJ stared at her a long moment. "Mom said she didn't have any family. Where have you been? Why haven't we seen you before?"

She wished she had a good answer for that question. "I live in Ohio. That's where we grew up."

"Did you have a mommy and daddy?"

"Yes. My mom was a secretary and my dad worked at an insurance company."

"What did Mommy do?"

Sophie laid a hand on Linney's shoulder, resisting the urge to hug her close. "She was a very good big sister." Until she walked out the door one day and never came back.

"How come Mommy never told us about you?"

Sophie chose her words carefully. "I don't know, Linney. Maybe she was busy being your mom. Sometimes people, even sisters, grow apart. But I've found you now. That's all that matters. I only wish I could have found you sooner."

"What do we call you?"

Katie's serious expression made Sophie smile. "Aunt Sophie would be nice."

"Come see our room, Aunt Sophie." Linney took her hand and tugged her forward. "You can see my dance costume. It has purple sparkles all over it. And I have lots of Barbies, too."

Katie grasped her other hand. "She doesn't want to see that stuff. I have lots of books and ribbons. I'm on the swim team. Mommy and Daddy came to every meet."

"I want to see everything."

The next hour passed in a flurry of dolls, books, impromptu dances and lots of sisterly bantering. Katie and

Linney weren't much different from Sophie and Madeline when they were young.

Sophie left the girls to play with their dolls and went in search of Zach. He might need help getting the food ready.

He was pacing while speaking on the phone when she entered the kitchen, his voice was tense as he spoke. "I need someone now. I leave tomorrow and someone has to be here to take care of the kids. I understand but—" He rubbed his forehead. "Fine. Yes. Thank you."

He shut off the call and tossed his phone onto the counter before seeing her.

"Is everything all right?" she asked.

Zach's shoulder's stiffened. "Yes. No. The nanny agency is having trouble finding someone to watch the kids this week when I'm on hitch."

"Hitch?"

"On duty. I fly helicopters. Deep water routes for an oil company out of Louisiana. Two weeks on, two weeks off."

"Who watched them the last time?"

"My aunt and uncle, but they've moved to North Carolina to be near their daughter." He ran a hand through his hair.

Sophie bolstered her courage. She had a solution but she doubted he'd like the idea, let alone agree to it. "I could stay with them."

Zach jerked his head up. "What? No. Not necessary. Something will turn up."

"By tomorrow?"

He set his hands on his hips, clearly wanting no part of her suggestion but he was also in a bind. "I appreciate the offer, but you don't know anything about the kids and what they need."

His harsh tone revealed his true feelings. "Don't you mean *you* don't know anything about me?"

He held her gaze a moment. "You're right. I don't."

"I'm very qualified. I'm a teacher so I know how to deal with many children. Plus I'm well qualified as a sitter."

Katie came into the room. "A babysitter? Do we have to? Why can't Aunt Sophie stay with us?"

Sophie quickly stifled the smile teasing her lips. Out of the mouths of babes. "That's a great idea. I'd love to take care of you while your uncle is working."

"Cool." Katie turned and ran from the room shouting. "Linney! DJ! Aunt Sophie is going to stay with us."

Zach was glaring. "You had no right to override me."

"I didn't. It was Katie's idea. Besides, you know it's the best solution. I'm here, I'm available and the kids want me to stay. What do you have against me, Zach?"

He fisted his hands on the counter. "You mean because you show up here out of the blue and assume you can just become part of our lives? I'm not comfortable leaving the kids with a veritable stranger."

"A nanny would be a stranger, too. What's the difference?"

He had no answer to that.

She certainly couldn't blame him for being protective of the children. "I want to do this, Zach. I won't let anything happen to them."

He obviously didn't like the option but he really had no choice. "Fine. You can move in tomorrow. I have to leave in the afternoon. That'll give you time to get the lay of the land."

Sophie couldn't withhold a happy smile. "You won't regret this Zach. I promise."

Chapter Two

Zach turned the burgers over on the grill on the back deck, staring blindly into the flames. How had he lost control of his life so quickly? Within a few hours his kids had embraced a total stranger, and he'd agreed to let her babysit them for a week while he worked. He should never have let this happen.

"Anything I can do to help?"

Zach glanced over his shoulder at the person responsible for the upheaval. "No. I've got it. They should be ready in a few minutes."

She came to his side, wrapping him in a light flowery scent. He tensed. He didn't want to get too close to this surprise aunt.

"The girls are so sweet. They showed me all their prized possessions."

He wasn't in the mood for small talk. "Yes, they are." He caught her gaze. "Why haven't we heard about you before, and why would Maddie deny having a family?"

She paled and crossed her arms over her middle. He

knew he was being rude, but he needed some questions answered if he was going to leave his kids with her.

"I wish I knew. She walked out of our house, supposedly on her way to college, but when our mother died a few weeks later, I couldn't find Madeline anywhere. She'd vanished and no one knew where she was."

Not the answer he was looking for. "Why didn't you try to find Maddie sooner? Why wait fifteen years? Did anyone file a missing persons report?"

She took a step back and he tempered his accusatory tone. He'd get nowhere by badgering.

"Because I didn't know where to start looking," Sophie said. "My father contacted the police and they tracked Madeline's car to Tennessee where she'd sold it. After that there was no trace." She took a deep breath and met his gaze. "I was fourteen. My mother had died, my sister had disappeared and my dad completely shut down. He dropped me off with my aunt and left. Two years later a policeman told me my father died in a fire."

Zach looked back at the grill, shoving the burgers around. He hadn't expected that explanation. Still, it didn't make sense. "Why would Maddie walk away like that? She never walked away from anything."

Sophie sank into one of the chairs at the patio table, on the deck resting her elbows on the glass top. "She and my mother were like oil and water. Everything Maddie did irritated her. Our parents were alcoholics. Dad was a sad drunk. He'd grow silent and unresponsive. Mom was a mean drunk and she took it all out on Maddie. I can understand her wanting to get away, but not why she cut me out of her life. We were close. I adored her."

The tremor in her voice filled him with shame. He

knew better than to judge others without knowing all the facts. "I wasn't aware of that. Maddie never talked about her past."

An awkward silence hovered between them. "The burgers are done," he said finally. "Why don't you get the kids?"

She nodded and went inside.

The meal passed pleasantly enough, except Zach found it hard to concentrate on his food. The girls were happily chatting with their aunt, who was obviously enjoying them, as well. Her smile was brilliant and the sparkle in her hazel eyes shone like a beacon. Giggles filled the air from all three of them. He didn't understand what was so amusing. It had to be a girl thing. But even DJ had shed his headphones and had added to the conversation.

Very puzzling. And irritating. What was it about this woman that made people gravitate to her?

He stood, suddenly filled with irritation and not understanding why. He began to clear off the table and the kids took the hint. They carried their dishes inside. Sophie brought up the rear. He sensed she wanted to talk.

"I should be going," she said. "I need to pack up a few things if I'm going to stay here while you're gone."

Her light fragrance swirled around him again. "Right." He took a step away.

"Thanks for lunch. I'll be back tomorrow and you can fill me in on what needs to be done while you're gone."

Zach opened his mouth to respond, but the kids walked in with serious expressions on their faces. "What is it?" he asked.

"We want a family meeting," DJ said, his arms crossed over his chest. Katie nodded, setting her hands on her hips.

Not what he'd expected. He'd continued his brother's practice of holding a family gathering whenever the children needed to discuss something. So far it had worked well, but with Sophie in the picture, he wasn't in the mood to play mediator. "Okay, we'll have one right before bedtime tonight."

Linney tilted her head back and emitted a whine. "No. It has to be *now*. It's 'peritive."

He saw Sophie lower her head to hide a smile. "'Peritive, huh?'"

Linney nodded. "We have to talk right now."

Sophie started to move. "I'll leave you to your meeting."

Katie spoke up. "No, we want *you* to be in the meeting, too."

"Me? Why?"

"'Cause you're our aunt."

Linney smiled up at her. "We love you."

Zach set his jaw. The last thing he wanted was for this stranger to sit in on their family meetings, but he knew he was outnumbered. Might as well give in or the pestering would go on forever. Besides, what would it hurt for her to see how things were done around here? "Fine. Family meeting called to order."

He motioned Sophie toward the family room. He followed behind, noticing again how much she resembled her sister, as if someone had sculpted a smaller, more delicate version of Madeline. Maddie had always worn her hair short but Sophie's light brown hair floated in waves just brushing her shoulders.

The children took their usual places for meetings. Linney and Katie sat at each end of the sofa, Zach in the middle, DJ settled on the coffee table. He was the usual spokesman. Zach waited while the boy gathered his thoughts.

"Mom's birthday is coming up and we want to do something to make it special."

Zach heard Sophie inhale sharply. Obviously, she was as stunned as he was. He wasn't sure what the children had in mind—perhaps a memorial of some kind, like planting a tree in her name. "All right. What's your idea?"

"Well, it's about the clothes closet."

Zach blinked. DJ's revelation landed with a thud in his chest. Madeline had been eager to start a community clothing store for the needy in town. She'd been deep into planning when the accident happened. She'd even purchased an old building to house the place. He'd kept up the payments on it simply because he wasn't ready to deal with putting it on the market.

He couldn't imagine what these kiddos had in mind. Surely the project died with their mother. "That's a very nice idea but I'm not sure—"

"*We're* sure," DJ spoke up. "She loved working at the church closet. That's why she wanted to make her own."

Linney nodded. "She had a store and everything."

"I know, but it's a big job."

Katie nodded. "We'll all help."

"The closet costs money and someone has to be in charge," Zach pointed out. "Your mom hadn't even started the remodel on the building, and I don't have time to take on that kind of job. It's a very nice idea but it's not practical."

Sophie cleared her throat. "I don't think I understand what a closet is?"

Zach leaned forward, resting his elbows on his knees. "It's a charity program where clothes are collected and then redistributed to those in need. Madeline ran the church community closet which was mainly for women reentering the workforce. She loved it, but thought it should be bigger so she bought the old bus station and planned to expand the charity. She was very passionate about it."

Sophie bit her lip. "Madeline was always thinking about others."

There was an odd tone in her voice that piqued Zach's curiosity. There was much more to the surprise sister's story and he wanted to know what it was.

Katie tugged on Zach's sleeve. "Please, Uncle Zach. We want to finish it. We want it to be Mom's birthday present. She really, *really* wanted to open the closet."

"I know, kids, but you have no idea what's involved. Someone has to be in charge, someone with experience setting up a charity like this. Not to mention the remodeling. Your dad was going to do that."

"Couldn't you do that? You used to work with Grandpa on the construction stuff. Dad said so."

"That was a long time ago. I'm not a skilled carpenter like your dad was. We'd have to hire a contractor and that's expensive."

The disappointment on the kid's faces broke his heart. Linney started to cry.

"But we want to do something special for Mommy. We miss her so much." Tears fell down Katie's face.

Zach reached for the girls, pulling them close. "I know, but it's not possible right now. Maybe next year."

DJ stood. "I knew you'd say no. You just don't get it."

Zach rubbed his jaw. He'd promised he would do anything for the kids but this was out of the question.

"I'll do it. I'll take over the project."

Zach stared at Sophie in disbelief. What was she thinking? Before he could refuse her offer, the kids erupted in joy.

"Thanks, Aunt Sophie." Linney scooted off the sofa and reached out for a hug, Katie clapped her hands, and DJ grinned and made a fist. "Cool."

Horrified, Zach tried to quell the outburst. "Hold on there. I haven't agreed to anything." Three voices rose in protest. He held up his hands to quiet them. He looked at Sophie, trying to ignore the disappointment in her hazel eyes.

"I appreciate the offer, Sophie, but the answer is no." He faced the kids. "I understand you want to see your mother's dream come true, and I'm very proud of you for such a nice idea, but it's not simply a matter of opening a store and filling it with clothes."

DJ frowned. "Why not?"

Zach set his hands on his hips. "It's a big job and your mom had only started to organize the closet. We have no idea what she had in mind."

"Yes, we do." DJ pointed to the desk near the back window. "She had all the plans on her computer. She talked about it all the time."

Zach rubbed his brow. "Maybe so, but there's the

matter of money. We can't afford to complete the closet, and I don't have the time."

Katie tugged on his sleeve. "But we can help. It's summer. We have plenty of time."

Sophie took a step toward him. "Zach, I really don't mind taking on a project like this. I actually have some experience in the area. I manage my aunt's small business."

Zach didn't appreciate being ganged up on, and he wasn't about to enlist the help of a relative who was basically a stranger. It was bad enough she was watching the kids this week. "Thank you, but it's out of the question." He stood. "This meeting is over. Maybe we can have a special meal on your mom's birthday. A cookout or maybe we'll drive down to the coast and spend the day at the beach."

Three very disappointed and angry faces stared back at him before they slowly left the room. Zach turned to Sophie, whose face revealed her own disappointment.

"That was the sweetest thing I've ever heard," she said softly.

"What did you think you were doing?"

She blinked, a flush appearing in her cheeks. "I just wanted to help, it's obviously important to them to honor their mother this way."

"Maybe so, but you have no idea what's involved and neither do they."

"Do you? Shouldn't we at least look into it? Maybe it wouldn't be that difficult to complete the project."

"Out of the question. Besides, I'm sure you're anxious to get back to wherever it is you came from."

"Ohio. And I'm in no hurry at all. In fact I planned

on staying here for several weeks. I wanted plenty of time to get to know the children."

Zach had reached the end of his patience. Showing up on his doorstep out of the blue didn't make her family. He tried his best to get control of his mounting frustration. "To be blunt, you're making things harder for me."

"By offering to help?"

"Yes." He set his hands on his hips. "I make a decision and you encourage them to ignore me and give them what they want. Ultimately I'm responsible for them. Sometimes that means making hard decisions."

"I want to make them happy."

He'd been touched by the children's suggestion and he hated to dash their dream, but he had to be sensible. "I feel bad, too. I wish I could grant the kids' requests. But it's out of the question."

Sophie tugged her hair behind her ear. "It's obvious the children aren't handling their grief well and working on this project could be a way to direct that in a more productive way."

The woman had her nerve. "They're dealing with their grief just fine."

"Really?" She crossed her arms over her chest. "DJ is sullen and angry. Katie is in denial, and Linney is like a little lost soul."

"Just what are you accusing me of?"

"I think you're a man who has no idea how to deal with three grieving children. And maybe a man who resents losing his carefree single life."

She'd hit the nail on the head and he didn't like it one bit. He was totally inadequate to raise his brother's children. Fear of failing them loomed over him every moment. It took all his strength to keep his comments to himself. "Thank you for your candor, but since you're a stranger here, I'll chalk your observations up to ignorance."

He knew by the look on her face he'd gone too far. This was the children's aunt. For their sake, he shouldn't alienate her.

She stiffened and reached for her purse. "I should go. Thank you for the cookout. It's been a long time since I had a grilled burger."

He lightened his tone. "Don't people grill up there in Ohio?"

"Yes, but I live alone and it's no fun to grill for one."

Zach kicked himself mentally. He understood only too well about being alone. He would have to remember that they were both new to this aunt and uncle thing. Her even more so than him. She'd just found out about Maddie's kids. He followed her to the door.

Katie and Linney saw them and ran to their aunt. Linney grabbed Sophie's hand and squeezed it against her little cheek. "Can't you stay longer?"

Sophie rested a hand on her head. "I'll be back in the morning. I'm going to be staying with you for a week, remember?"

"Come back for breakfast. Uncle Zach makes the bestest waffles ever."

Zach grinned at the compliment. At least he was doing something right.

"Sounds good to me. I love waffles."

DJ spoke up suddenly. "We use real maple syrup, too."

Sophie smiled at him over her shoulder. "Wonderful. That's my favorite. It must run in the family." She winked at him and the boy actually smiled back. First one Zach had seen in days.

After a round of hugs and a few kisses from the girls, Sophie left and Zach took the first calm breath he'd had all day.

What had the woman been thinking, offering to spearhead the closet project? It was ridiculous. One thing was very clear. He didn't want the kids getting too attached to the surprise aunt because they'd be hurt when she left. They didn't need any more loss in their lives.

"I just love her." Katie spoke in a breathless tone before plopping onto the sofa with a dreamy expression.

"I'm happy 'cause now I have an aunt *and* an uncle," Linney declared before she skipped off outside. DJ, as usual, had retreated to his room.

The sudden silence allowed a flood of uneasy thoughts into Zach's mind. Why was being a parent so difficult? He wished he could go back to being the favorite uncle. The guy who swooped in once in a while and delivered presents and took them to the beach. Now he was more like their parent, and the fun stuff would be Sophie's job now.

Somehow he'd find a way to make up to the kids for turning down their idea. After all, he was partly to blame for the accident that took their parents. If he'd flown them home like he was supposed to, they wouldn't have been driving and there wouldn't have been an accident. Being named as guardian had been a blessing and afforded him a chance at redemption.

He'd devote his life to his brother's kids, and maybe in time he could forgive himself for his mistake.

Sophie pulled up at the house the next morning, unable to keep from smiling. She would be spending the entire week with her nieces and nephew. The thought gave her more joy than she'd known in a long time.

The idea was even sweeter since she wouldn't have to deal with Zach. He was overly protective of the children and she suspected he was resentful of how quickly she had bonded with them. She'd pegged him as self-centered and too quick to squash the children's ideas.

That was probably unfair. Zach had been hit with an unexpected relative and a surprise request from the children all at the same time. To be honest, she shouldn't have offered to take on the closet project without discussing it with him first. She'd almost retracted her statement, then she'd looked at the children's faces. They wanted to honor their mother and—she soon realized—so did she. Completing her sister's dream would be a way to reconnect and bridge the gap for all the lost years. Perhaps she wasn't the only one being selfish.

The front door opened before she could knock and Linney smiled up at her.

"I didn't think you'd ever get here."

Katie ran and hugged her the moment she entered the kitchen and Lumpy nuzzled her hand again, begging for some love.

"It smells good in here." The aroma of bacon and coffee fueled Sophie's appetite. She settled at the large kitchen island where Zach was mixing the batter.

"Mommy and Daddy used to fix us waffles all the time."

Sophie gave Linney a hug. "When we were young, your mommy and I used to make them on weekends."

Zach's phone rang and he picked it up, his expression tightening. "I have to take this."

He walked off, unaware of the dejected faces of the children.

Linney pouted, resting her chin on her fists. "He'll talk forever and we'll never get our breakfast. I'm hungry."

"Me, too." Sophie stood and picked up the bowl of batter and opened the waffle iron. "Let's get started. I'm sure Uncle Zach won't mind." Within minutes Sophie was filling three plates with hot waffles and basking in the smiles of her family.

Zach entered the room and stopped in his tracks. "You started without me."

DJ stabbed another bite of waffle. "We were hungry."

Linney nodded and smiled. "And look! Aunt Sophie showed us how to put strawberry preserves on them. It's yummy."

Lines formed on his forehead. "I thought you liked real maple syrup."

Katie nodded. "But this is good, too."

Sophie could tell he was troubled about something more than syrup. She decided to bide her time until they could talk privately. She suspected that it wouldn't work to her advantage to be too inquisitive. Zach would only clam up and retreat.

Becoming part of her sister's family was harder than she'd expected.

* * *

Zach leaned against the kitchen counter, draining the last of his coffee from a mug with a picture of a brown Lab on the side. His house felt off-kilter this morning. It had taken him weeks to find a comfortable routine with the kids and the surprise aunt had shuffled it around in only twenty-four hours. She'd been dragged off by the girls after breakfast, leaving him alone and feeling like the kid who wasn't picked for the ball team.

A tapping on the back door drew his attention as Hank entered, a big smile on his craggy face. Zach wasn't surprised. His part-time boss usually showed up when there were waffles to be had. He motioned for his friend to come in, nodding toward the remaining stack of waffles.

Hank helped himself to a cup of coffee and took a plate from the cupboard. "I didn't expect the new aunt to be so pretty."

Zach frowned. "How would you know?"

Hank took a seat at the table, drowned his waffle in syrup and grinned. "She was outside on the deck when I arrived. She's a softer version of her sister, don't you think?"

Zach set his jaw. "Is she? I hadn't noticed."

"Right." Hank drew the word out with a skeptical grin. "She seemed very nice. I like her."

"You can have her."

Hank speared another bite of waffle, then washed it down with a gulp of coffee. "So what's your beef?"

"No beef. I don't know her."

His friend nodded. "How did the kids take to her?"

"Like a long-lost relative."

Hank chuckled under his breath. "I get it. She's bonding too quickly with the youngsters and that makes you nervous."

Zach gripped his mug between his palms. "She's going to stay with them while I'm on hitch this week."

"Whoa, that was fast."

"I didn't have a choice. There wasn't anyone else."

Hank shrugged a shoulder. "It's only a week. And Paula and I are right up the street. What could happen?"

"I don't know. That's the problem."

Hank patted him on the back. "Don't worry. I'll check in on them every day to make sure she hasn't kidnapped them or anything."

Zach jerked his head up. "Do you think she would do that?"

"Whoa. Chill, buddy. I was joking. You're getting yourself all worked up for nothing. Don't anticipate trouble before it happens."

Zach tried to ignore his friend's comment, but even after he'd left, the words rolled around in his head, sending roots deep into his already troubled thoughts. Was that why the aunt had shown up? She wanted to legalize her rights as a relative? They'd already disagreed on the closet. Could she use that against him and prove he wasn't a suitable guardian?

He emptied his mug in the sink, then fisted his hands on the counter. It wouldn't be hard to do. He messed up royally every day. It was his worst nightmare. Leaving a stranger to take care of his kids. It was going to be a long week.

Chapter Three

Sophie stepped into the master bedroom later that morning, unprepared for the emotional tidal wave that engulfed her. Her pulse raced, sending blood surging through her ears. How was she supposed to stay here? How could she sleep at night without thinking about her sister being in this room?

She sank onto the edge of the bed, her knees too weak to hold her. A picture of Madeline and her husband sat on the nightstand and she picked it up, tears stinging her eyes.

Why had she abandoned her? She could understand not contacting their mother, but why hadn't she at least let Sophie know she was all right? They'd been close even though they'd been four years apart in age. But what did she know about her sister really? Nothing. Her eyes scanned the room again. But maybe now, in Madeline's home and surrounded by her children, Sophie might find the answers she longed for.

And she needed answers. She needed family. Now more than ever.

"Aunt Sophie. I have a surprise for you."

Sophie looked up as Linney appeared in the doorway clutching flowers in her little hand.

"I picked them for you."

Sophie quickly wiped the moisture from her cheeks and smiled. "Thank you. I love them." She reached out her hand but Linney's smile faded and she took a step backward. "What's wrong, sweetie?"

"I don't want to go in there."

It took Sophie a moment to grasp the significance of the situation. Linney knew it was her parents' room and she was reluctant to enter. Sophie's heart ached. Poor little thing. Sophie understood only too well the emotional impact of being in this room.

"This is a very nice room. I'm sure your mommy and daddy were very happy here."

Linney mulled that over for a moment. "I guess so." Slowly she entered the room, her free hand clenched into a tight fist.

Sophie's throat tightened. "It makes me sad to be in this room. It makes me miss my sister very much. Is that why you don't want to come in? Because it makes you miss your mommy and daddy?"

Linney nodded, her eyes wide.

"Would you like to help me unpack? You know where everything is and I don't."

"Yes, ma'am. Mommy said we should always help others."

Sophie took the flowers from her hand and laid them on the bed. "Your mommy was a very nice lady." Sophie fought the knot in her throat. She pulled a pair of shoes from her suitcase. "Where should I put these?"

"There's a special rack in the closet. Mommy put hers there but all her things are gone now. Uncle Zach gave them to needy people." Linney took them from her, then hurried ahead to the door beside the bathroom, opening it and placed them on a shelf. "You can hang your clothes in here, too."

"Good idea. Thank you for helping me, Linney. Your mommy would be very proud of you. You look like her." Linney was a miniature of her mother down to the brave tilt to her chin.

"That's what Daddy always said. He called me his little Madeline. Linney for short."

"Linney, are you okay?"

Zach stood in the doorway, glancing between Sophie and Linney, a deep scowl creasing his forehead and a dark shadow of concern in his brown eyes.

She nodded. "I'm helping Aunt Sophie unpack."

"That's very nice of you." He motioned her toward him, clasping her hand and pressing her against his side in a protective manner. "Why don't you go downstairs and feed Lumpy? His bowl is empty."

Zach didn't speak again until the child was out of earshot. "What are you doing?"

The harsh tone in his voice sent a twinge of alarm along her skin. "What do you mean, what am I doing?"

He took a step toward her, making her heart jump. "Linney is a very sensitive child. She's still trying to adjust to losing her parents. Forcing her to enter this room is cruel and I won't—"

She held up a hand. "Excuse me. I didn't force her to do anything. She entered on her own."

He set his jaw. "No. Linney refuses to come in here."

"She did at first, but we talked a little and then I asked her to help me unpack, and she agreed. There was no coercion involved."

Zach's jaw flexed. "Did you offer her candy or something?"

Sophie tried not to be insulted. He was obviously concerned for his niece, but he had no right to accuse her of doing something hurtful. "No. I talked to her about her mom and dad. That's all."

Zach shifted his weight. "I don't want you to push the kids to talk about their folks. That's my job."

Sophie raised her chin. "Are you? Talking to them?"

The scowl on his face deepened before he spun on his heel and walked off, leaving Sophie scolding herself for speaking so bluntly. There was something about the man that got under her skin and made her want to challenge him.

That had always been Madeline's response to things. Challenge and attack. Maybe Sophie was more like her sister than she realized.

Zach went in search of his youngest niece, taking a few calming breaths as he went. The woman was infuriating. Leaving her in charge of his kids for a week was a mistake. He hated to think of the damage she might do, but he had no other option. He found Linney in the kitchen poking a straw into a juice box.

"Are you okay, Linney Bug?"

She smiled up at him. "Yes, sir."

He squeezed her hand. "I'm sorry your aunt made you go into your mom and dad's room."

"She didn't make me. I wanted to go in."

He'd tried multiple times to coax the little girl into the room, hoping to overcome her fears, but he'd failed each time. "You did? Why?"

"She asked me to help her unpack since I knew where everything was, so I did. Mommy always said we should help others."

"It didn't upset you, to be in there?"

"A little, but Aunt Sophie needed my help."

"You know you can talk to me about your mom and dad whenever you want."

She shook her head. "You don't like to talk about them. Can I go outside now?"

"Yeah." He ruffled her hair as she ran out the back door, leaving him with an odd discomfort in the center of his chest. The child was right. He didn't like talking about Madeline and Dean. He owed Sophie an apology. He'd been convinced she'd dragged his niece into a room she dreaded. Somehow the woman had managed to break through the child's fear and grief simply by talking.

Talking. It apparently worked for everyone but him. When he had attempted a conversation about their parents, the kids had become more upset than before so he'd backed off, assuming that when they were ready they would talk to him. Maybe they were ready now.

How was he supposed to know?

Sophie had accused him of resenting the responsibility of the kids. If he was perfectly honest, he did miss the freedom of coming and going as he pleased, the satisfaction he found in his career. But all he had to do was look at those three sweet faces and he knew whatever he'd given up was nothing compared to having them in his life.

He wasn't looking forward to making his apology. Neither was he looking forward to being gone all week. What else would Sophie talk them into? She had a connection with them that he obviously lacked. He couldn't deny there was something warm and compelling about Sophie. He could understand why the kids were drawn to her.

All he could do was hope that a week managing three kids would be too much for her to handle and she'd be ready to pack up and go home.

He held on to that thought as he said goodbye to the kids a short while later. Katie and Linney stared at him with worried expressions. DJ looked indifferent. Zach wished he could find a way to connect with the boy but so far all his attempts had failed.

"We'll miss you, Uncle Zach."

"I'll miss you, too, Linney Bug."

"Have fun flying your helicopter." Katie hugged his waist. "Be careful."

"I will, Katie Belle. You be good for your aunt."

She nodded happily. "We will. It's going to be so fun having her here for a whole week. We're going to do all kinds of cool stuff."

Zach didn't want to think what that cool stuff might be. The sooner he went to work, the sooner he'd be back home.

He met Sophie's gaze. "Take good care of my kids."

She lifted her chin in a defiant gesture. "I will. I love them, too."

He held her gaze a moment. Was it possible to love

kids you'd only known for twenty-four hours? He'd have to take her word for it. And do a lot of praying between now and when his hitch ended.

Sophie rinsed her coffee mug and placed it in the dishwasher. So far her first full day alone with the children was going well. Zach left right after lunch yesterday. She knew he hadn't been thrilled about leaving her in charge. He'd left her detailed instructions on their daily routines, a schedule of activities, a list of chores and an emergency phone number list that covered half the population of Blessing.

She couldn't fault his actions. She would have been anxious, too, if the situation were reversed. She may have reservations about some of his parenting decisions, but there was no doubt that he loved their nieces and nephew.

"Aunt Sophie."

She turned around as the children came and stood in front of her. They exchanged conspiratorial glances. DJ spoke first. "We want to talk about Mom's closet."

Katie nodded. "We have to talk Uncle Zach into it."

Sophie's heart warmed at their love and devotion, but antagonizing Zach wasn't wise. "That's probably not a good idea. Your uncle was very clear that he had neither the time nor the money for the project."

DJ exhaled an exasperated grunt. "But he didn't look at all Mom's stuff. She had it all worked out. Maybe we can find a way to do it that won't cost so much."

Linney clasped her hands tightly together under her chin and gave her a pitiful expression. "Please."

"It was important to Mom."

DJ's pleading tone punctured Sophie's conviction. Going against Zach was risky. He could forbid her to see the children ever again, but they were her nieces and nephew, too, and the community closet had been important to Madeline. And now it was important to Sophie. "Well, I suppose it wouldn't hurt to look over her files."

The girls squealed and gave her hugs. DJ offered up his palm for a high five.

"But on one condition. We don't say anything at all about this to your uncle. I need to look over all the information first and come up with a plan. But I'm not promising anything. Is that understood?"

"Yes, ma'am." DJ grinned and handed her a laptop.

"What's this?"

"Mom's computer. It's all on there." He opened it and with a few taps on the keys located the folder for the closet.

Sophie clicked on the icon and a stream of files appeared. "There must be thirty files here. This will take time to go through."

DJ emitted a soft chuckle. "Yeah, but Uncle Zach won't be home for another six days."

It took the better part of two days to go through all Madeline's information. From what Sophie could tell, her sister had done all the prep work. Permits, licenses, taxes and approvals from the town had all been filed and approved. Even the details of the remodel had been addressed. All that remained was the mortgage on the building. It was considerable. The monthly payments would put a strain on any family budget. Sophie could better understand Zach's concern.

If only there was a way she could help with the payments herself, but she doubted he would agree to that. She'd put her aunt's gift shop and her home up for sale, but money from that wouldn't be available until the properties sold, which could be several months. This project needed to get underway quickly. The children needed this to move forward. And school would be starting up before long. If only there was a way around the money issue.

Money! Of course. Madeline had money. Lots of it. Pulling out her own tablet, Sophie quickly scanned her personal files. There it was. The savings account her aunt had set up for Madeline after she'd sold their parents' home. Sophie had used hers for college tuition. Since Madeline's whereabouts had been unknown, Aunt Billie had put the money in a savings account until she returned. There should be more than enough to pay off the mortgage and remove Zach's biggest objection.

She sent up a prayer. This might just convince Zach to launch the community closet. But first she had some investigating to do.

Sophie stepped out onto the front porch the next afternoon and took a seat in one of the rocking chairs. Her head was throbbing and her vision blurred from staring at the computer for the last several days, but her hopes were rising. She had everything she needed to proceed with the closet, provided she could get Zach to accept Madeline's inheritance. She hadn't mentioned anything to the children in fear of getting their hopes up.

A friendly shout caught her attention and she glanced

up to see a tall, dark-haired woman come toward her from across the street.

"I just wanted to say hello. I'm Rachel Burkett. My daughter Bailey is Linney's best friend, and my son Carter is on DJ's ball team. Are you the nanny Zach hired?"

"Actually, I'm their aunt. Sophie Armstrong. Maddie's younger sister." Sophie braced for the surprise that was sure to come. She wasn't disappointed.

The woman's eyes widened and her jaw dropped. "I had no idea she had a sister. She never mentioned it and we were best friends."

"Maddie left home as soon as she was old enough and we lost touch over the years." She saw the curiosity bloom in Rachel's dark eyes, but Rachel only nodded and took a seat in the other rocker.

"I'm sorry to hear that. If there's anything I can do or if you have any questions, don't hesitate to ask."

"As a matter of fact, I have one question. What do you know about a community closet my sister wanted to start?"

Rachel grinned. "Everything. I was her assistant. Well, not really, but I helped her think it all through. It's a shame it won't happen now. It would have been a real blessing to the community. Why do you ask?"

"The kids approached Zach about completing the project. They want to do it as a birthday memorial for their mother. It's very important to them."

Rachel clasped her hands over her heart. "That's the sweetest thing I've ever heard. Maddie would be so proud of those kids."

"Well, their uncle said no. He claimed he didn't have

the time or the money for the project. The children were heartbroken. I even offered to take charge of the whole thing and help the kids, but he said I was undermining his authority."

Rachel sighed. "It might appear that way but you have to realize Zach went from being a carefree single guy to a parent of three kids overnight. Financially he must be stressed."

"Maybe, but how was Maddie going to get it done if money was tight? She must have had some kind of plan. I've been through all her files but I couldn't find any financial information."

"Those records were probably on Dean's computer. He was going to do all the remodel work himself. She was also counting heavily on volunteers. We had a long list of people who were going to help."

"From where?"

"Church. I'm the president of the women's ministries at Blessing Community, but there were others from around the town. We have no shortage of civic-minded folks in Blessing."

Rachel started the chair rocking. "Your sister was involved in many organizations in town. She spearheaded several of them. She was a bundle of energy. Sometimes I wondered if all her running around and busyness wasn't a way for her to avoid something painful in her life. Something she was avoiding."

Sophie's heart skipped a beat. Like avoiding her sister, her family? She filed that comment aside to examine later.

Rachel chatted a few minutes longer, then left leaving Sophie with renewed hope. She had a financial resource to tap into and people to call upon to help. How could Zach say no now?

A glance at the clock Saturday morning reminded her that Zach would be home in a few hours. She was nervous about bringing up the closet conversation, but she'd vowed to stand her ground. It was too important to the children. She hadn't told the kids what she'd discovered but she'd reassured them that she was still looking into things.

The week had gone by quickly and with few glitches. The children were all cooperative and helpful. DJ had even spoken out loud more this week. Linney had introduced her to all of their Barbie dolls and Katie had set her books aside in favor of asking questions about her mother.

Sophie had found comfort in talking about her sister with the kids. Being in her home hadn't proved to be as difficult as she'd expected. Yet there'd been moments when she'd remember she was sleeping in her room, or when she looked at the children and her heart would grieve. So many years lost. She hoped eventually to understand why Maddie had cut Sophie out of her life.

She took her seat on the sofa as the children wandered in after cleaning up the kitchen. Katie sat beside her with a book in her hand, snuggling close. DJ turned on the TV and Linney stretched out on the floor to watch with him, using Lumpy as a pillow.

For the first time in her life Sophie understood the meaning of the word *content*. She closed her eyes, willing the feeling to penetrate deep into her being so she could remember it forever, because she was only here temporarily.

Zach had called as often as possible during the week, and Hank had stopped by each day to check on them. Her main concern now was whether Zach would allow her to remain in the house or ask her to return to the inn. She hoped not because she liked being part of this family.

Unfortunately, it didn't matter what she thought. Zach had the final say. He was the kids' legal guardian. The old sense of disconnection washed through her but she tamped it down with memories of the time she'd had with the children this week. She smiled remembering the giggles they'd shared when they'd played a silly board game, and the evening on the front porch in the rain talking about Madeline.

Zach parked his car in front of the garage and shut down the engine, glancing at the house. What would he find after being away for a week? When they'd spoken on the phone, the kids had promised him they were enjoying being with Aunt Sophie, and she had assured him everything was going smoothly. In addition, Hank had confirmed all was well.

As he stepped into the family room, the sound of the TV was all he heard. Everything looked normal. The kids were in their usual spots, with the exception of Sophie who was snuggled up with Katie on the couch.

The sight brought an unexpected warmth into his chest. She looked comfortable and at home, but that was probably because she looked like her sister and he'd seen this domestic picture before, whenever he'd come to visit. But Sophie wasn't her sister. Madeline's home was always full of activity and excitement. Sophie's presence exuded a quiet peacefulness.

He exhaled a sigh of relief. Everything was just as he'd left it. "I'm home."

Linney jumped up and ran over to him. "Uncle Zach! I missed you."

He smiled and picked her up in his arms. He'd missed them, too. More than ever.

DJ glanced over his shoulder, pulling his attention from the TV briefly. "Hey, Uncle Z."

Katie leaned forward on the sofa and waved. "We're glad you're back." She grinned, glancing at Sophie.

Something in her expression worried him. Maybe he had cause for concern after all. "I'm glad to be back."

Sophie met his gaze, a welcome light in her hazel eyes. "I hope you had a good week."

He took a seat in the leather recliner. "So everything go okay while I was gone?"

DJ shrugged. Linney smiled and explained how she and Sophie had played board games, and Katie launched into a list of things she'd learned about her mother.

Zach relaxed, sinking into the warm comfort of being surrounded by his family again. As much as he hated leaving his job with Sandler Oil, he knew it was the right thing to do. He needed to be with his kids. They needed him.

To be honest, this last hitch had forced him to face a few truths. A fierce Gulf storm had made his last trip to the oil rig platform the most harrowing of his career. With a full load of souls on board his helicopter and a packed cargo hold, the winds had fought against him. It was the first time he'd actually doubted his ability

and made him realize that he had more than himself to
think about now.

Unfortunately, flying was all he knew how to do.

Zach was mindlessly watching TV later that evening
when Sophie approached him.

"Do you have a minute? I'd like to discuss something with you."

He'd learned long ago that when a woman wanted
to talk, it usually meant trouble. "If it's about you staying here at the house, that's up to you. I'll be flying a
few charters for Hank and giving flying lessons at the
airfield. So I'll still need someone to watch the kids."

"All right. I don't mind staying on for a while, but
are you really going to continue flying?"

"It's what I do. What I've always done."

"Yes, but don't you think it's a bit risky now? If
something happened to you, these children would have
no one."

Zach refused to get into an argument about it with
her. "What did you want to talk to me about?"

Sophie bit her lip and her hazel eyes clouded. He
knew it. Something had happened while he was gone.

She sat on the edge of the sofa, her hands clasped
together. "The children approached me about the closet
project."

Zach exhaled sharply. "I thought we had that all settled."

Sophie nodded. "But I've been looking into Maddie's files and—"

The woman had some nerve. "Who gave you permission to do that?"

"The children, actually. DJ gave me Maddie's laptop with all her information."

He started to protest but she held up her hand.

"Please hear me out before you start shouting."

"I don't shout," he said loudly. When he realized the irony, he felt his cheeks heat.

"Madeline had everything ready to go on the closet," Sophie explained. "She was going to start as soon as she got back from their trip."

Zach's heart dropped. Only she never came back.

Sophie cleared her throat and continued. "All that's left to do is to prepare the building. She even had a list of volunteers lined up."

He lowered the footrest with a quick kick. Sophie flinched but he didn't care. This was no concern of hers. "Maybe so, but that still leaves the cost of remodeling and that's not in my budget right now."

"What if I could provide the money for the building?"

"Absolutely not. I'm not accepting any donations from you. This is a family matter."

Even though he'd been hurtful, Sophie pressed on. "Not *my* money. Maddie's. Money left to her from the sale of our parents' house. It's been sitting in an account collecting interest all this time and it's more than enough to pay off the mortgage."

Zach shook his head. "It doesn't change anything. I still don't have the time to dedicate to this project. I have to work, and right now I'm unemployed. Besides, we don't know what Madeline wanted to do with that closet."

"But we do. She had it all outlined, down to a detailed floor plan for every hanging rack, fixture and bench."

Zach stood, shaking his head. "Sophie, I appreciate you wanting to help the kids. I do, too, but this is not a good time for this."

He saw her chin lift the same way Maddie's had when she'd made up her mind about something. Dean had always told him once his wife's chin went up he might as well jump on the train or be run over.

"Really? I think it's the perfect time. Working on this closet, finishing their mother's dream, could be the thing that helps them come to terms with their grief. It's something tangible and hands-on they can do."

"The kids are dealing just fine."

"I disagree." She crossed her arms over her chest. "They are all hurting and lost. This could make the difference. Think of what's best for the children, Zach."

Zach shook his head. "I am thinking of what's best for them. Taking on a project this size is too much for them right now."

"No, you're not." DJ came toward his uncle. "You're only thinking about you. You think we're just kids so we don't know anything, but we do. It was important to our mom. I wish she was here instead of you!"

DJ marched out the back door, slamming it behind him. Zach sighed. "I'd better go talk to him."

He stepped outside to find DJ sitting on the back porch steps, shoulders hunched and head bowed. Zach sent up a prayer for divine guidance. He had no idea how to talk to the boy.

He eased down beside his nephew, waiting.

DJ stared straight ahead for several moments, then

finally he said, "I was supposed to go to work with Dad this summer. He'd been teaching me carpentry and how to use some of his power tools. We were going to start by working on Mom's store."

Zach's chest tightened. "I didn't know that."

"You don't know much."

The rude tone in DJ's voice would normally earn him a stern reprimand, but Zach sensed this was something he needed to let slide. "You're right. I don't know much about being a dad or taking care of three kids by myself or even how to keep the family together. That's why I can't afford any big projects like the clothes closet until I understand more about how to take care of you and your sisters."

"The closet was important to Mom and Dad. It's important to us. Why won't you let us finish it? Aunt Sophie said she would help. She cares about us and what we want, but you don't. You only care about your dumb flying. Dad always said so." DJ stood and went back inside.

It wasn't the first time Zach had been accused of being single-minded. His parents had continually pushed him to expand his interests. His former fiancée, Elaine, had broken off their engagement three years ago because she said he loved flying more than her. He hadn't been able to tell her otherwise.

He got up, intending to check on DJ. Zach knew he'd hide in his room, don his headphones and fume for a while, but he'd get over it. Wouldn't he? Or was this closet thing bigger than Zach realized?

The truth chased him all through the night, robbing him of sleep. The kids' request couldn't be ignored or

dismissed any longer. DJ had made him see how important it was to the three of them. Now he had to swallow
another huge chunk of pride and agree to the project.

Sophie would be happy. She was taking over and he
didn't like it one bit. For now he'd focus on what the
kids wanted and let Sophie come along for the ride. He
hated to admit it but this project might be good for the
kids. Sophie was probably right. Lord knew they needed
help and Zach was failing miserably.

Chapter Four

The July heat was already intense at nine in the morning Monday when Sophie and the family arrived at the old bus station Maddie had bought for the clothes closet. Getting used to the humid Mississippi weather would take some time.

Sophie waited while Zach unlocked the door, admiring the historic architecture. The station, with its art deco design, would be the perfect setting for the closet. The exterior glazed bricks were a sky blue shade with curved corners and glass block windows. A large canopy jutting out from the side once offered protection from the elements for passengers. The only thing missing was the large sign identifying it as the bus station. Her heart raced at the thought of working in this 1920s building. It wasn't a huge structure but was definitely the perfect size for the clothes closet.

The children pushed past Zach, eager to see inside. Sophie stepped over the threshold, glancing around the large empty space. Up until now the closet had been an abstract concept. The reality sent a chill through her.

Somehow she had to make the dream come true for her sister and the children.

The responsibility settled heavily on her shoulders, unleashing all her insecurities as she moved farther inside. The building had ended life as a station years ago. Madeline had noted that it had been divided into two offices for a time, then remodeled into a travel agency, but had stood empty for over a decade now.

The space was dim, dusty and filled with odd debris. Sophie walked slowly through the wide space that had probably been the waiting area of the bus station. A long wooden bench divided with armrests sat against the back wall, along with several cabinets of varying sizes. On the far left wall, the ticket counter remained intact, its wire cage fronts and mouse holes standing ready to pass tickets to eager travelers.

She could hear the kids as they explored the old building. Zach had wandered off on his own.

She turned and started toward the opposite end of the old structure, her imagination soaring. She could see why her sister fell in love with this place. All the plans and drawings Madeline had gathered started to come to life. Still, Sophie had to wonder how long it would take to turn this rundown space into a functioning store.

Katie dashed past, a big smile on her face. "Isn't this the coolest place?"

Zach followed right behind, a frown on his brow. "If you say so."

DJ glanced up. "What are we supposed to build here?"

"Beats me."

Clearly Zach wasn't feeling the excitement about the

building. "I know exactly what has to be done," Sophie reassured her nephew. "Maddie had it all drawn out."

Zach exhaled a skeptical breath as he turned to face Sophie. "If you ask me, this place needs to be leveled."

"Oh no. It's perfect. I can see why Maddie chose it."

Zach scowled. "You have a very vivid imagination."

She laughed and the sound echoed around the empty space. "No imagination needed." She lifted the roll of blueprints she'd brought along. "I know exactly what Maddie wanted. It's all here in blue and white."

She moved to a small table and brushed off the dirt and dust. Unrolling the large paper, she placed her small purse in one corner to hold it flat. "See, the checkout counter will be right back there, this area will be the women's dressing rooms, the men's will be back there and the large area will be clothes racks. The other corner will be an office and a small break room. That back room will be for collecting and organizing the clothes."

Zach came over and leaned in to study the plans. "These are professionally done. That'll make the remodel easier. The plumbers and electricians will be grateful."

Sophie smiled and glanced around the space. "I can't wait to see Maddie's dream come true. It's going to be wonderful."

She met Zach's gaze, her breath disappearing from her lungs. His dark eyes were warm and kind. Not filled with his usual defensive glare. It softened his angular features, and gave his stern mouth an intriguing tilt. Even the ever present scowl on his forehead had softened. If she hadn't known better, she'd mistake the light in his eyes for attraction. But that was ridiculous.

When he continued to stare, she grew concerned. "Is something wrong, Zach? Is the project too big? Maybe we can rework it here and there. Scale it down."

"No. It's fine. As far as I can tell from one glance."

Relief mixed with excitement washed through her. "When do you think we can get started?"

"Like I said, I'll have to look things over, calculate materials, contact a few people. We might be able to start by the end of the week."

"Not tomorrow?"

"Hardly. Besides, I have to teach at the flight school the next few days."

Sophie fought her disappointment. She didn't want to waste a moment. "I'll be glad to get things started if you'll tell me what needs to be done."

Zach shook his head. "You've done enough. Now it's up to me." He rolled up the blueprints and slipped them back into the tube.

She didn't like his dismissive tone. "Please don't shut me out. I'm supposed to be managing all of this. Remember?"

"Would you like a nightly debriefing?"

She ignored the sarcasm in his voice. "That would be wonderful. You can tell me what needs to be done, I'll handle it during the day and we can go over everything each night at dinner. That way the kids can be kept in the loop, too. It's their project after all. Thanks, Zach."

His scowl was back. "I'm going to look around a bit more. Give a shout when you're ready to leave."

Watching him walk away, her concern grew over how their partnership would play out. She had a bad feeling that communication with Zach would be a challenge. How would Maddie have handled this situation? She would have stood up for herself, which is what Sophie would have to do if she was going to make her sister's dream a reality.

Zach's mind shifted like a revolving kaleidoscope. Somehow she'd solved one problem by producing the blueprints and created two others by reminding him she and the kids were planning on being involved. Just when he thought he'd regained control, it was yanked from his grasp.

"This is a big project, pal. You might need some help."

Zach whirled around, smiling as he recognized the voice of Buck Sullivan, his brother Dean's lead carpenter and foreman. "Hey, man. It's good to see you."

They shook hands. "I saw your car out front and thought I'd stop in and check things out. I've been wondering about this place since Maddie bought it."

Zach exhaled a deep sigh. "Yeah. If it was up to me, I'd scrap the whole thing, but Maddie's sister and the kids are determined to finish what she started."

"I think that's great. Shows initiative."

Zach grimaced and set his hands on his hips. "Right."

Buck grinned. "Could you use some help?"

"Are you offering?"

"Sure. Your brother was into this closet thing. He talked about it a lot. I can find some time to lend a hand. My way of paying tribute to him. He was a great guy. A good man to work for."

Zach slapped him on the shoulder. "That would be great because Madeline's sister wants to manage this whole deal and she doesn't know the first thing about remodeling. And I could use some guidance. It's been a while since I've done any serious construction work."

Sophie returned and Zach introduced her. "Buck, this is Maddie's sister, Sophie. Buck worked for my brother for years."

Sophie extended her hand and Buck took it, holding it a bit longer than necessary. "I'm pleased to meet you. You're a nice surprise."

Sophie chuckled softly. "A surprise maybe, but I'm not sure how nice it is. So you worked for Maddie's husband?"

Buck smiled and nodded. "His oldest employee. He and Maddie were good friends. They're greatly missed."

"I wish I could have met him."

"I told Zach I'd be happy to help out. This project was important to Dean and Maddie."

Sophie smiled. "Oh good. I can use someone with experience to help me keep things on track. I must admit I'm feeling overwhelmed."

Buck pulled out a business card. "That's where I come in. I'll walk you through everything. Call me if you have any questions. I'm between jobs at the moment so I'm available anytime."

Zach glanced at the two of them. They had forgotten he was even there. "I have the blueprints over here, Buck, if you'd like to take a look at them." He walked away.

Buck followed but not before saying something quietly to Sophie. Zach had never known the man to be so chatty. He spread out the blueprints again, grateful for the assistance of a skilled builder. It would make the project go faster and he was anxious to get it completed quickly and with little fuss.

As he and Buck went over the specifications, Zach's confidence grew. His plan for the remodel and Buck's advice were in line. Apparently he hadn't forgotten all his father had taught him. They set a time to get together and lay out a schedule for construction and decide which subcontractors to hire. They shook hands and Buck walked off.

Zach rolled up the blueprints again and went in search of the kids. He didn't want them hanging around here too long. It wasn't safe. He found them and Sophie at the front door talking with Buck. Sophie was giggling like a schoolgirl.

He didn't remember Buck being so amusing. He'd always found him the stern, serious type.

Buck ruffled Linney's hair, gave DJ a fist bump and smiled at Katie before shaking Sophie's hand. Again. And holding it a little longer than necessary. Again. Maybe he didn't need the man's help after all. Zach could manage on his own. No need to keep Buck from a paying job.

The children were bouncing off the walls with excitement. Today was demolition day at the station and they were ready to break down walls and tear up floors. No matter how many times Sophie explained it to the kids, they still believed that they were actually going to swing sledgehammers and pry up wood flooring. She had a plan in place to let them do a small amount of physical destruction but not like they'd seen on those home shows on TV.

Zach entered the kitchen as she was starting the dishwasher.

"What has the kids all hyped up? They're acting like it's Christmas Eve or something."

She chuckled softly. "It's demolition day."

Zach narrowed his eyes. "You're not thinking they're going to help, are you? Because that's out of the question."

Sophie dialed back her irritation. "They have to be part of this, Zach. That was the whole point in reviving the project. We can't leave them at home while all the work is being done."

"I'm not having them around a demolition site. It's dangerous."

"I'm aware of that. But I have a plan." She picked up a plastic sack and fished out a pair of safety glasses. "I found these in children's sizes and I bought hard hats, too."

Zach shook his head and crossed his arms over his chest. "That's not going to work."

"Just hear me out. I already checked with Buck and we picked out a spot in the southwest corner of the store where they can break through a wall and pull up a few loose floorboards. They can't get hurt and it'll make them feel like they really contributed. They'll only be there a short while and I'll take them over to Rachel's after so they won't be around the dangerous stuff. I wouldn't allow that."

"Good. Wait. You talked with Buck?"

She nodded. "He's been helping me understand the remodeling process. Oh, I meant to tell you, we picked up the building permit, and the Dumpster should be delivered this morning."

"Buck is on the ball, I see."

"Actually, I arranged that," she clarified. Zach didn't look happy. She'd expected him to be relieved, or maybe grateful.

"We're ready."

The children darted into the kitchen each holding a bright green hard hat. Linney had hers strapped onto her head. She kicked her foot out. "I'm ready."

Sophie winced at the stern glare Zach shot in her direction. Thankfully he didn't comment. He just said, "I'm going on ahead. See y'all there."

Zach walked out and Sophie began to think her attempts to keep the children involved in this project might be harder than she expected. She admired his desire to protect the children, but they had to feel they had a part in their mother's project or it wouldn't mean anything. Surely he understood that. And if he didn't, she'd make it abundantly clear to him. After all, this was about the children honoring their mother.

Zach was talking with Buck when she and the children arrived at the old station, and he didn't look happy. He was probably still complaining about letting the children do minor demolition. He didn't seem to understand that they needed to participate in this remodel as much as possible. She was convinced there were plenty of things they could do that would make them feel part of things and not put them at risk.

Buck looked over as they entered and waved, gesturing toward the wall they had determined was a good place for the children to smash around without getting hurt. She handed each a small hammer and instructed them to secure their hard hats and safety glasses, then gave them directions on what to do.

With big smiles they attacked the wall with their hammers, making little holes in the drywall. Buck and Zach came to stand beside her. Buck rested his hands on his hips, smiling at the children's enthusiasm. Zach stood stiff and disapproving.

DJ yanked off a large chunk of drywall and let out a whoop of triumph.

Zach stepped forward. "Good job, kids, but that's enough for now. We'll finish the rest."

DJ lifted his glasses. "Aunt Sophie said we could pull up some floors, too."

Zach shot a glare in her direction. She ignored him.

"Right in here. I'm not sure the girls are strong enough but we'll see." She handed DJ and Katie a scraper. Buck demonstrated with a larger one.

Buck patted DJ on the back. "DJ, why don't you scrape and the girls can pick up the pieces and toss them in the trash can."

Their enthusiasm for the work didn't last long. Linney plopped on the floor and Katie dropped her scraper. "This is hard."

DJ leaned his arm on his scraper handle. "I want to keep going. There's lots more to get up. Besides, I'm here to work, not horse around."

Sophie collected the girls' hard hats and safety glasses and went in search of Zach. "I'll take the girls to Rachel's. Be right back."

"No need. Buck and I can handle it. I think there's a couple more guys coming soon to help."

"I have some design decisions to make and I can't until the demolition is done," Sophie countered. "I'm in charge here, remember. At the very least, I can clean up debris."

"Uncle Zach, I want to stay," DJ protested. "I can't learn anything about carpentry sitting at home."

Sophie could see Zach determining his response. "DJ, I'm not sure there's much you can do right now. You can be of more help later."

DJ frowned. "No! You promised to teach me the job. Like Dad was going to do."

Sophie's pulse raced. "Zach, if you promised, then you have to follow through."

He glanced between them, then sighed. "Fine. I guess you might as well hang around and learn from the ground up."

Sophie sighed in relief. For a moment she'd feared Zach would go back on his promise, and the one thing she couldn't tolerate in others was breaking a promise. It was the ultimate betrayal in her point of view.

Linney hugged Zach's neck, then kissed him on the cheek. "Thanks for letting us help with the demolition today, Uncle Zach. It was really fun. We took down a whole big wall." She spread her arms wide.

Zach chuckled. It was hardly a whole wall, more like a small patch, but he wasn't about to ruin Linney's joy. "You did a good job, Linney Bug."

"Can we do more tomorrow?"

He pinched her cheek and smiled. "Probably not. But next time we need an extra hand, I'll let you know."

"Good. I'm going to help do lots of stuff on Mommy's closet 'cause I'm bigger now."

Zach's heart twisted. She was getting bigger every day and he wished with all his being that her parents were here to see it.

"Good night." She dashed off down the hall and pounded up the stairs.

Zach rested his head against the back of the recliner and closed his eyes, only to open them again when he caught a whiff of Sophie's subtle perfume. He always knew when she was close. He opened his eyes and waited for her to speak.

She took a seat at the edge of the sofa. "We accomplished a lot today."

He nodded. "It helped that we had a couple of volunteers show up."

"Our little volunteers had fun helping to take down that wall."

"That's all the girls have been talking about."

"They were thrilled to help. Thank you for letting them participate. It was very important to them."

Zach caught her gaze. "Yeah, well, I'm glad you had it all worked out ahead of time. There wasn't much danger of them getting hurt on that wall."

"That's what Buck thought. And look how much happiness that small job gave the children."

Zach pressed his lips together. Since when was Buck an expert on kids?

"How did DJ do after we left?" she asked. "He hasn't said much."

"He worked hard. Mainly helping clean up debris." He'd been pleased and proud of his nephew's work ethic.

"He's really determined to learn and follow in his father's footsteps."

"I know. I'll teach him all I know but Dean was the master carpenter." Zach had often marveled at his brother's talent. He could do amazing things with wood, from building a kitchen cabinet to a small jewelry box. He hoped DJ had inherited his brother's ability.

"So what do we tackle tomorrow?" Sophie shifted back on the sofa, drawing her feet up under her. She reminded him of Katie when she was reading a book. She always curled up that way.

Zach lowered the footrest and stood. "Nothing. I have a couple of flight lessons to give at the airfield tomorrow and I have a charter scheduled for a week from tomorrow." He started to walk away, willing himself to ignore her sweet intriguing scent.

Sophie rose from the sofa and followed him. "Friday? That's Katie's birthday."

"Is it?"

"Yes. She mentioned it several times while you were away. I'd like to do something special for her. I know she'll be feeling her parents' loss deeply that day."

"Fine with me."

"Will your charter flight be over by dinner time?"

"It should be. It's an up-and-back to Boise."

"That's up in Idaho. That's really far away. Won't that take a long time?"

"Not at five hundred miles per hour."

Katie hurried into the room and looked up at Sophie. "Did you ask him about my birthday yet?"

She slipped her arm around the girl's shoulders. "Yes. You're all set."

"Cool. Thanks, Uncle Zach. I have the day all planned out. We're going to have a big breakfast, then Aunt Sophie and Linney and me are going to go shopping and then we're going to get a chocolate cake with lots of chocolate icing, and Aunt Sophie is going to make Mommy's favorite meal for supper, then we'll all watch my favorite movie. Promise you'll be here?"

"I promise. I wouldn't miss it for anything." His heart tightened. Her first birthday without her parents. It wasn't right. But he would do all he could to make it a good day.

Katie hugged him tight, reluctant to let go. He'd learned that it was a sign she was struggling so he held her close until she was ready to release him. She smiled up at him, her sweet face filling him with a swell of love.

"We're going to decorate the whole house. It's going to be spectacular."

She hurried off and Zach glanced at Sophie. Her expression wasn't one of happiness as he'd expected. She looked irritated. He raised his eyebrows.

"Don't make promises you can't keep, Zach. Promises are very important to children."

"I'm aware of that. I wouldn't have told her I'd be here if I thought I couldn't be."

"I hope not. Broken promises are never forgotten." She left the room, leaving him wondering what she'd meant. She was clearly upset but he wasn't sure why. There'd been a tone in her voice that concerned him. It was tinged with sadness. What had happened to her? There was a lot he didn't know about the surprise aunt. Maybe it was time to start learning.

* * *

Sophie retreated to her room, her heart rate gradually slowing. Zach said he would honor his promise to Katie and be home for her birthday party. Would he? Did he have any idea how important promises were to children? Did he understand that a broken promise was a wound that never healed? She had a lifetime of broken promises to prove it.

Closing her eyes, she sent up a prayer that Zach would keep his promise. When she opened her eyes, her gaze landed on the well-worn Bible she'd found in the small side table in her sister's room. The book was filled with scribbles, notes and underlined passages. Sophie had never seen a Bible like this. In her aunt's home, the Bible wasn't to be defaced in any way. Aunt Billie considered it a holy item and to be treated with reverence. Maddie's Bible bore testimony to her daily reading of the Scriptures and the insight she gained from the verses. It was also giving Sophie a glimpse into her sister's thoughts.

Lifting the leather-bound volume, she settled in to continue her nightly reading. Spending time in the Word was always a comfort to her, but seeing the notes in Maddie's own hand and meditating on the passages she'd highlighted gave her hope that she'd find the answers to some of her questions about her sister's actions and motives.

So far she'd found no explanation for the long silence between them. However, the proof of her true heart was revealed in her children, and the more time Sophie spent with them, the more she understood what was important to Maddie: her family.

It's what Sophie hoped to gain, as well. Her recent infection and resulting hysterectomy made having a child of her own impossible, but she held out the hope of being part of Maddie's family. And God willing, one day she'd find someone who would love her and perhaps consider adopting a child with her.

Closing the Bible, she prepared for bed. She had too much to do now to waste time dwelling on the past. She had to decide on the decor of the store and had plans to execute for Katie's eleventh birthday party. Everything had to be perfect. Her niece was a sweet young girl and she deserved a special party.

Sliding under the covers, Sophie curled on her side, her gaze resting on the novel she was reading. She and Katie were alike in one way. They both devoured books. Aunt Billie had called Sophie a bookworm.

That was it. The perfect theme for her niece. Books and reading. Tugging the covers up to her chin, she smiled, her mind already swirling with ideas. She couldn't wait to get started. She'd make sure it was perfect. Nothing would go wrong. Unless Zach broke his promise.

But their uncle was a good guy. He wouldn't fail his niece.

Early the next morning, Sophie's cell phone ring tone woke her. She had no idea why her friend Angela was calling.

"Is it too early? I forget that Mississippi is on Central Time."

Sophie curled onto her side. "No. It's fine."

"I'm dying to know how things are going down there."

"Okay. The children are wonderful. We're getting along great, but their uncle is another matter."

"Uh-oh. Tell me more. What's he like?"

"Serious. He seems to have a permanent scowl on his face and he resents any comments or suggestions I make."

"He sounds like an ogre."

"He's not. I think he's overprotective of the children. I don't blame him for that. It's his resistance to me being part of the family that's troublesome."

"What's he look like?"

Sophie smiled. Angela was all about the attractive quotient. "He's tall, a little over six feet, I guess, with broad shoulders, trim and fit. His hair is dark brown, almost black. He keeps it short. Brown eyes, intelligent, probing, but they soften each time he looks at one of the children."

"Uh, girlfriend, he sounds yummy."

"He's attractive, I guess, but I'm not looking for any kind of relationship and I'm positive I'm not his type."

"How do you know?"

"I just know. My only concern right now is the children. I just want to find a way to connect with Zach so I can be part of the family. I'm so tired of being alone, of having no one."

Sophie hated the break in her voice. Thankfully, Angela understood. Was there any way Sophie could penetrate Zach's shell and not feel like a stranger who was intruding into the children's lives? "He doesn't even know the children's birthdays."

"Maybe he's not family material."

"Then maybe he shouldn't be their guardian."

"Give it time, Sophie. You'll work it out."

Sophie ended the call hoping her friend was right.

Chapter Five

Zach slid his phone into his pocket, then headed out
the back door a few days later. He'd hoped to have more
charter flights from Hank, but his regular pilots were
covering the schedule which left little to a part timer
like him. At this rate he'd never earn a paycheck. And
working as a flight instructor for the county airfield
didn't pay well either. He needed a full-time job.

He'd applied for several helicopter openings locally.
The position with the forestry company had already
been filled. That left the energy company and the pilot
job for the county hospital helicopter emergency evacu-
ation team. He'd made follow-up calls to both but there'd
been nothing to report. Hopefully something would
come through soon. The children's future was secure
thanks to their parents' life insurance, but the day-to-
day expenses had fallen on him. His savings were suf-
ficient for the time being but they wouldn't last forever.
He needed a job.

A flying job.

Thankfully the remodel at the closet kept him occupied, and teaching DJ the ropes had been more enjoyable than he'd anticipated. He was especially looking forward to working today. Sophie had taken the three kids to the dentist, which would tie her up for most of the morning. She would bring DJ by this afternoon, which worked out well because Zach had a meeting with Buck to go over the plumbing situation in the morning.

Zach always got more done when she wasn't there. Her questions about how things were done were annoying and her mere presence a big distraction. He kept looking for her, wondering where she was and what she was doing, just to make sure she wasn't disturbing anything, though it didn't seem to bother Buck much. He appeared to enjoy explaining the construction process to her.

The shop was buzzing with activity when Zach arrived. Buck was leaning over the blueprints in what would become the office with Owen Young, the plumber, beside him. He'd expected someone from Ace Plumbing Company to be here since he and Buck had agreed to use them as a subcontractor, but Owen was retired now.

Owen turned and smiled. "Hey, Zachary. Good to see you."

Zach shook his hand. "I'm surprised to see you, sir."

"You'll be seeing lots more of me for a while," Owen said. "I'm going to be roughing in your new pipes."

Buck grinned. "He called me last night and offered his services and materials. I couldn't turn him down."

"That's great. Any place we can save money is a good thing."

"Well, I know how important this place was to Dean

and Maddie and it'll be a valuable asset to the community. When the tire plant closed last year, a lot of people lost their jobs. A place like this can help folks get back on their feet."

Zach gestured toward the two men at the back of the building. "And those guys?"

"Part of my crew. They wanted to help, too." Owen gave him a pat on the back and joined his men.

Buck slipped his hands in his pockets and smiled. "I've had calls all morning from people who want to help. Jeffery Logan has offered to handle the landscaping. Mrs. Fuller has arranged for lunch for the workers each day, and the church youth group is available to help whenever."

Zach ran a hand through his hair. "I had no idea people even knew about this place."

"Apparently, Maddie had lined up a long list of volunteers. Your sister-in-law was a very persuasive woman."

"So I'm learning." He'd thought he knew his brother and his wife but he was beginning to think he didn't know them at all. How had he been part of the family and not been aware of their plans?

Buck scratched his chin. "That's the good news. Now for the bad."

Things had been going smoothly so far. Zach wasn't surprised there were a few problems cropping up. "Lay it on me."

"Asbestos. That back room is covered in it. It'll have to be professionally removed. I've already talked to the remediation company and they can start the day after tomorrow, but this could hold up construction for almost a week."

Zach clenched his jaw. A delay like that could have a domino effect on other parts of the remodel. Plus, if he got a job now, it would make finishing the closet nearly impossible. He'd forgotten how unpredictable the contracting business could be. He had no idea how his brother had survived the job for so long.

"I'm hoping they'll seal off that part of the building and allow us to work in the other areas for now," Buck went on. "In the meantime, we'll stay out of that section."

One week into the remodel and they'd already hit a big snag. Zach didn't want to think about what else might come up.

Three cars were parked in front of the old bus station when Sophie arrived midday. The vehicles didn't belong to subcontractors. They were personal cars. Zach had called and told her DJ didn't need to come to the closet today and that he'd explain when he saw her. Taking the tile samples from the back seat, she hurried inside hoping nothing was wrong.

"There you are, Miss Sophie. I'm glad I caught you."

Evelyn Roberts was the last person Sophie expected to see in the middle of a dirty, dusty construction zone. The older woman was the most fastidious person she'd ever met. Never a hair out of place or a speck of lint or dust on her anywhere. Rachel had introduced them at church last week during the after-service fellowship gathering. "Miss Evelyn, how nice to see you."

"I brought a nice hearty lunch for everyone. My

friend Velma and I set it up in the back corner. Please help yourself."

"That was very thoughtful. I'm sure the men appreciate your kindness."

Evelyn smiled and smoothed the front of her skirt. "Well, I wanted to help but there's not much I can do other than pray, of course. I'm not very handy. My Arnold always took care of that. There wasn't anything he couldn't repair."

Sophie walked with Evelyn to the makeshift lunch buffet. The men were making quick work of the food as fast as Velma could replenish it. Zach waved and came toward her.

"Thanks again, Miss Evelyn, for the lunch." Zach said. "It's a nice break from the fast food we've been getting."

"No trouble. I'm happy to help. I'm eager to see this closet up and running. Maddie was a good woman, and this was so important to her."

Sophie watched the woman return to the table and exchanged surprised looks with Zach. "I never would have believed I'd see her here."

"Me either. She's not the only one who stopped by to help." He gestured behind her where two elderly gentlemen, deacons at the church, were sweeping up the floor. "They offered to come by each night and clean up."

"Amazing. I had no idea. I mean, I know there's a list of volunteers but I didn't really expect them to show up."

Zach caught her gaze. "Don't people show up in your world?"

There was no easy answer to that question. She pulled her gaze from his dark eyes and looked over to the food on the table. "I'm more used to them disappearing."

Zach sighed softly. "Well, Blessing is an unusual place, and this closet has, for reasons I don't understand, drawn people together. Not that I'm complaining. We can use all the extra help we can get."

Tears welled in Sophie's eyes. "It was Maddie. She had a way of drawing people in, getting them caught up in her plans and her dreams."

"I remember. She had an endless source of enthusiasm."

Sophie felt the fierce tightening in her chest. Her stomach knotted. Sweet memories of Maddie mingled with anger, flooded her mind like a tidal wave. Pivoting on her heel, she hurried outside, taking refuge behind the building where she could cry, away from curious eyes.

Why had her sister made time to help all these other people but could never find the time to reach out to her? Had she hated her so much? She pounded her fist against the old bricks.

"Sophie."

The soft voice pierced her grief. She froze. Glancing at the ground, she wiped her eyes and turned away from Zach's presence. Why couldn't he leave her alone?

"Is everything all right?"

"What do you think?"

She heard him exhale slowly. "Sorry. Is there anything I can do?"

She turned to face him. "Can you bring my sister back? Can you tell me why she left me behind and never called or wrote? Can you explain to me why she ignored my very existence?" She covered her mouth as sobs rose up in her.

Zach reached out and touched her arm. She pulled away and felt a strange moment of regret. She ached for comfort but accepting it from Zach terrified her.

"I wish I could answer your questions. Truth is, I didn't know Maddie that well."

Sophie looked at him. "She was your sister-in-law."

"Exactly. My brother's wife. Not my close friend. I loved her because she was a good wife to Dean and a wonderful mother to their children. She was kind and thoughtful and fun, but she didn't confide in me. We didn't share our secrets."

"Your brother never said anything?"

"No. He hinted that she sometimes became sad and melancholy for no reason, but those moods were short lived and infrequent so he dismissed them as unimportant."

"Do you think she was regretting leaving me?"

"Maybe. I don't suppose we'll ever know."

"But I need to know. I have to understand." She fought a new wave of sobs.

He rested his hand on her back, gently steering her back around the building. "Why don't you go home? There's not much you can do here. Time alone might do you good."

She shook her head. "I've had fifteen years alone. Now I need to keep busy. I have tile samples I need to look over." She walked ahead of him and opened the front door. She turned. "Thank you, Zach. I appreciate your help."

"Any time."

Did he mean that? She hoped so. She had a feeling he really did understand her situation, more than she'd expected. Strange, because she hadn't figured him for the sympathetic type.

For the first time since she'd met Zach, she entertained the thought that he might actually become a friend.

Zach set his hands on his hips, chewing the inside of his mouth. He hated feeling useless, and finding Sophie in tears behind the store had made him feel worse than useless. He didn't know what to say or do. Did he walk away and leave her alone? Or did he try to fix it for her? Walking away had seemed cruel. Besides he couldn't stand to see her so upset. So he'd offered to help.

He entered the store, glancing around to see where Sophie was, and found her in the front room spreading tile samples on the floor. She seemed okay now. She'd wanted to keep busy and he should, too. There was still a lot to do before they could start moving clothing in.

Zach tried to lose himself in framing the walls of the dressing rooms, but he kept looking over his shoulder for Sophie. When he saw her leave, his tension eased. Maybe now he could concentrate on his work and not on the way Sophie's tears had affected him.

"You're awful quiet. You seem a bit preoccupied." Buck leaned against the wall and stared at him.

Zach dropped his hammer into his tool belt, searching for an explanation. He could use some advice but didn't want to betray Sophie's confidence. "I guess I am. A friend of mine is having some trouble and I'm not sure how to help."

"Sophie?"

"No." His quick reply was a dead giveaway and he knew his friend would catch that.

"Right. Well, sometimes all we can do is stand back and wait. Guys like to jump in and fix stuff, but when it comes to women, it's best to just be patient and let them come to you."

He knew Buck was right but he couldn't get the sight of Sophie in tears out of his mind nor the pain in her voice when she talked about her sister. He was beginning to see that finding Maddie, and learning why she'd cut ties with her family, was so important to her. He couldn't imagine not knowing where Dean was for years on end.

Sophie had a big heart, as big as her sister's, but she managed it differently. Sophie went about her tasks quietly, steadily, with little fanfare. Almost as if she didn't want anyone to know she had done something kind. Maddie had always been about getting attention. The more people she could attract, the more she could accomplish. He liked Sophie's way better.

Buck tilted his cap back on his head. "You told Sophie about the asbestos?"

"No. I haven't found the right words. She's going to be upset."

"You'd better find them quick. It's not the kind of thing you can hide."

Zach practiced telling Sophie about the asbestos issue on the way home. She'd left the store without speaking to him so he had no idea if she was still upset or not and the last thing he wanted to do was upset her again.

He entered the house quietly, hoping to get a feel for

her mood. She was curled up on the sofa, her back to him when he stepped into the family room. Her head was bowed as if reading a book. As he approached, he saw it was a sketch pad in her lap and she'd drawn a picture of Lumpy sprawled on the floor, his big sad eyes looking pitiful. He smiled. She'd captured the dumb dog perfectly.

"I didn't know you were an artist."

She gasped and tried to cover her work. "Oh, I didn't hear you come in."

He rounded the sofa, nudged Lumpy from the cushions, then sat beside her, holding out his hand for her sketch pad. Reluctantly she gave it up. "You're very talented." He started to turn the page. "May I?"

She shrugged. "I guess so."

The next sketch was of the shop, filled with clothes racks and people shopping. The next was of Katie and Linney at the breakfast table laughing.

Sophie reached over and took the book back from him. "It's just scribbles. Drawing helps me relax."

"I'm impressed."

She hugged the book to her chest as if it were something precious to be protected.

He took the hint and changed the subject. "Where are the kids?"

"Linney is over at Rachel's playing with Bailey. Katie is up in her room planning her party, and DJ is—"

Zach finished her sentence. "In his room."

She grinned. "Yes. He was very disappointed that he couldn't go to the shop this afternoon. He likes working with you. He says you're a good teacher."

"He said that?"

"Yes. He says he wants to be a contractor like his father."

Zach rubbed his chin. "When did he talk to you?"

"We talk every day in the car on the way home. He's really enjoying working on the project. It's good for him."

Zach stood and moved to the recliner. DJ talked to Sophie but wouldn't talk to him. Zach had tried repeatedly to draw the boy out, even on the job site, but all DJ could manage was a grunt or a nod.

Zach looked at Sophie. What was it about her that made people want to bare their souls? He'd felt it himself, a strange compulsion to unload his worries. She had the ability to talk to others, something he obviously lacked. Talking was supposed to smooth out all his issues, but when it came time, he could never find the words.

"What happened?"

He jerked his thoughts back into place. "What?"

"At the shop. Why couldn't DJ come to work this afternoon?"

He couldn't put it off any longer. "Asbestos. We'd thought since the place had been remodeled several times over the years that it would have been discovered by now. Apparently the back room had never been touched so now we have to have it remediated and that'll take about a week to complete."

"Is it safe to be in the building?"

"We're hoping they can seal off that part and we can keep working but we won't know until they look it over. We may have to stop work for four or five days."

"But this will put us behind schedule." A frown creased her forehead. "We have such a tight deadline."

Zach didn't want to think about that but it was obviously foremost on her mind. "I know. I'm afraid we might not be done before you have to leave."

Sophie's hazel eyes darkened. She stood up and said, "I'm sure that suits you just fine, but don't get your hopes up. I'm not leaving until this project is completed. I wouldn't do that to the children." She strode off, her shoulders stiff and rigid. He heard the front door close with more force than usual.

What had he said? He'd expected her to be upset by the delay but not by his comment.

Maybe she was upset because he hadn't said how much he admired her drawing? He stood and went to the kitchen to fix something to eat. He found a plate in the fridge with his name on it. It wasn't the first time Sophie had done something thoughtful. She was always thinking ahead, making sure everything was in order, prepared for the next day, the next step. Maybe that was it. She was upset that they hadn't discovered the asbestos sooner.

What else could it be?

DJ entered the room and took a handful of cookies from the ceramic container on the hutch. "What's wrong with Aunt Sophie? She looked steamed."

"We had a setback at the store today. We won't be able to work on it for a week."

DJ slumped onto one of the kitchen chairs. "Why not?"

"Asbestos. It has to be removed and we might not be able to work in the store until it is."

"But you were going to let me put up some walls and use the big nail gun."

"There's other things we can do. We need to start on the cabinets. We'll work in your dad's shop. I'll pick up the lumber first thing tomorrow, and we can have most of them built by the time we can get back into the store."

"Okay. Will you show me how to use the chop saw?"

Zach's blood chilled. He wasn't sure his nephew was old enough to attempt that. Though he had a good grasp of the other power tools and he had shown a lot of common sense and safety awareness. "We'll see."

What would Dean have said? How did a parent know when a child was old enough to try something new and potentially dangerous? DJ was nearly thirteen. Which responsibility took precedence? The one to keep a child safe or the one to allow them to venture into new areas of discovery? How did you know which one to choose?

Sophie would probably know. She seemed more aware of what was age appropriate for each child. Probably the teacher in her, but he wasn't going to seek her advice and admit that he had no idea what he was doing when it came to parenting his kids.

Hank's comment was never far from his thoughts. If Sophie found him unfit as a guardian, she could petition for custody. He wasn't going to allow that to happen.

No one would take his family away. Not even the sweet Sophie.

By the time Sophie had crossed the street and knocked on Rachel's door, her irritation had started to fade but not enough to hide it from her new friend. "Oh my. What's wrong? You look upset," Rachel said.

"Not really." Sophie shrugged. "Okay, maybe a little."

"Come in and I'll fix you a glass of sweet tea. I don't think Linney is ready to go home yet. They're dressing their dolls for a fancy ball."

Sophie sat in the window seat in the breakfast room that looked out over Rachel's backyard and pool. "It's nothing."

Rachel raised her eyebrows. "I know that tone. It usually means man trouble."

Sophie blinked. "How did you know?"

"I use it all the time when Kyle messes up. What has Zach done to ruffle your feathers?"

Sophie slowly turned her tea glass, trying to decide on a place to start. "Zach is anxious for me to leave. In fact, he can't wait for me to pack up and go home."

Rachel took the seat across from her. "Oh, I doubt that."

Sophie shook her head. "I thought we'd reached a level of compatibility. Things had been going well since we started working on the closet, but now I think he's only tolerating me. He was never happy about me getting involved in the project to begin with."

"Do you *want* to go back to Ohio?"

"No. There's not much reason to return. I've put my aunt's gift shop and house up for sale, and I have few friends there anymore. They've either moved away or they have families that keep them busy. I had pinned my hopes on becoming part of my sister's family. I thought I might move here permanently. But now that seems like a foolish notion."

Rachel patted her hand. "Not at all. The children love you. The girls talk about you all the time and even

DJ has admitted you're cool. That's high praise from a teenage boy."

Sophie grinned. "I know the children care, but Zach is the one in charge of their lives. And I have a way of… irritating him."

"Maybe he's jealous of how quickly the kids took to you."

"I doubt that. But the bottom line is, I'm here for the children and to make sure the closet is finished. Anything else is secondary. Once the store is up and running, I'll worry about the future. I'm just hoping Zach will agree to let me visit as often as I can. I'll miss the children so much."

"I must admit I'm puzzled by your assessment of Zach. He's always been such a nice man. Madeline spoke so kindly of him."

"If she was here, everything would be so much simpler…or maybe not. I'd still be a big shock to everyone." Sophie took a sip of tea. "It might help if I understood why she told everyone she was an orphan."

Rachel shook her head. "I can't imagine, but…"

Sophie met her gaze. She had a feeling her friend was about to tell her something important. "But what?"

"Your sister was a sweet and generous woman but she had a troubled spirit. I never figured out what it might have been, but now I'm wondering if it had something to do with you."

"I don't understand."

Rachel paused a moment before continuing. "Maddie would sometimes fall into a dark mood that could last several days. I usually left her alone and respected her privacy, but there was one time when she came here needing to talk. She confessed that she had done something she regretted, but she didn't know how to fix it. When I asked her to explain, she only shook her head and admitted that she should have faced the problem long ago, but the longer she put it off, the harder it became and now it was easier to ignore it. She said some mistakes you can't go back and fix or forgive."

Sophie's breath caught in her throat. "Do you think she was talking about me? That she regretted leaving her family?"

"I don't know. It could have been or it might have been something else entirely."

Rachel's revelation replayed in her mind the rest of the evening. Had Madeline wanted to reach out? Why would she not follow through? Surely she knew how much Sophie loved her, how much she missed her. If only they could have talked.

After settling the children in bed, Sophie retreated to her room, not bothering to say good night to Zach. Her feelings were still stinging from his *go back home* attitude.

Unable to sleep, she curled up in the arm chair and opened her sister's Bible, idly leafing through the pages. A highlighted passage on forgiveness caught her eye. It wasn't the first one she'd noticed. Many of her sister's notes focused on forgiving others.

Unwilling to explore that thought, she picked up her sketch pad and opened to one she'd done of the family. She'd drawn it from memory one night after a particularly lovely evening together. They'd had a hearty meal, then gathered in the family room to watch a movie. It was such a special moment she'd been compelled to capture it on paper.

Katie was curled up with a pillow, DJ draped over one of the chairs, Linney and Lumpy as usual on the floor snuggled close. Zach was observing it all from his recliner, his expression one of deep love and contentment. While usually he was a very guarded man when it came to his emotions, his love for his nieces and nephew was visible for all to see. Sophie could never doubt how much he loved them. There was more to Zach Conrad than she'd expected and she wanted to know him better.

Unfortunately she probably wouldn't get the chance.

Chapter Six

Zach fixed a cup of coffee the next morning and carried it out to the front porch, joining Sophie on the swing. It was a beautiful morning with low humidity. A rare thing in late July in Mississippi. "Good morning." Sophie gave him a half smile in response. Whatever had offended her last night still festered, though he was still puzzled by what he'd said that could have upset her.

The awkward silence stretched on and he searched for a topic. "I've been meaning to ask you how this charity closet thing works. Do people just come in and take what they need?"

"No. If all they need are clothes on their back, there are other service organizations that offer that. Clothing is more than a basic need. In this day and age, image is important to fit in socially, to build self-esteem and sometimes to advance a career. Maddie's shop will provide that for those who may have fallen on hard times or need a hand up to get back on track."

"So do they pay for these clothes?"

"No, but we'll keep track of those who take advantage of the ministry. Maddie had already made arrangements with the social services in town for referrals. She also designed a system for keeping track of who comes in for clothes, how many people are in the family, their ages and what they need."

"So people can't just walk in off the street and buy stuff."

"No. And we'll only be open a few days a week. But if someone does come by and they aren't referred to us, then we'll register them and go from there."

Zach leaned forward, smiling. "Sounds like you have every detail worked out."

"Not me. Maddie. She was amazing. All I had to do was put things in motion."

"You're really enjoying this, aren't you?" Her delight was reflected in her eyes and her smile.

"I am. I feel like I'm working alongside her, bringing her dream to life. I just wish she was here. It would have been fun and maybe it would have brought us back together and she could have…"

"Have what?"

Her smile vanished and the light in her eyes dulled. "Nothing." She stood. "I have things to do."

Zach blew out a breath. Why were women so hard to understand? He stared into his coffee cup. He didn't like being at odds with Sophie. They'd been getting along well. The closet project had brought them and the kids together. He hoped once the delay over the asbestos was done and they could get back on schedule, things would return to normal.

He'd grown comfortable with normal. He wasn't sure how things would be once Sophie went back to Ohio.

The thought of her leaving Blessing left an odd emptiness in the center of his chest. He'd gotten used to her being around, helping with the kids and at the store.

He had to remind himself that she had a life up north. He doubted she'd be interested in staying in a small town like Blessing. Once the closet was up and running, she'd probably be anxious to go back home. Seeing how upset she'd been over her sister, he doubted she'd want to stay here surrounded by the painful memories.

He stood and walked to the porch railing, staring out at the lawn. She'd become the aunt who visited on holidays. Would that be enough? For the kids? He knew how much they loved her, how close they were becoming. A holiday relative wasn't the same as one who was around all the time. And Sophie would want to be close to the kids.

He dumped his remaining coffee into the bushes below. On the other hand, her leaving would be hard on the kids. It might be better if Sophie left as soon as the closet was open rather than let the kids get any more attached to her. Wouldn't it?

Sophie strolled the church grounds, now covered with picnic tables and lawn chairs all occupied with happy members. Today was the annual family cookout. Several large grills were cooking delicious burgers, hot dogs and other delicious food. From what she could see, they were having a hard time keeping up with the demand.

The children were off with their friends enjoying the activities, and Zach had gathered with some buddies near the grill chatting. She drifted off to the sidelines for a little quiet time. Maddie had always been energized by people and activities. Typical extrovert. While Sophie enjoyed the gatherings, after a while she needed a little time away to regroup.

Naomi Horvath, the church secretary, had told her earlier that the church had offered one of its rooms to house the clothing donations. The generosity of this town never ceased to amaze her. No wonder Maddie had been happy here.

Pastor Miller passed by and smiled. "Aren't you eating, Miss Sophie?"

"I'm heading over to the food now." She watched him stroll off, the words of his sermon earlier still lingering in her mind.

He'd spoken on forgiveness, referencing many of Maddie's underlined passages. She'd taken it as a nudge from the Lord to do some serious soul-searching. Forgiveness was something she'd struggled with since Maddie had left. Perhaps it was time to examine her own heart before she could move forward.

A few days later, Sophie waited impatiently for the coffee to finish brewing, then quickly poured herself a cup, added a little sugar and cream and savored the first sip. Mentally she ran through her birthday party checklist one more time. She'd ordered Katie's cake from the bakery in town and picked up the gummy worms for the ice cream topping. Her only other objective for the day was to keep Katie occupied by decorating the house. She was so excited about her eleventh birthday party tomorrow, she was talking a mile a minute and bouncing off the walls. Sophie hoped working at the closet today would give her something else to think about.

The asbestos had been removed and work could finally resume. Drywall was scheduled to start going up in the front part of the building and Buck had told her the plumbing and electric would be ready for inspection midweek.

But today she was preoccupied with Katie's party. Every day she prayed that her presence would ease the children's sorrow in some small way. Her mom and dad wouldn't be at Katie's party, but her aunt and uncle would be, and she hoped that was enough. She was determined to make the day perfect for Katie.

She looked up as Zach strolled into the kitchen and poured a cup of coffee. "Good morning."

He nodded and joined her at the table.

"What are you working on at the closet today?"

"DJ and I will finish the checkout counter and hang the doors on the dressing rooms."

"He'll be glad to get back to work. How's he doing?"

Zach smiled and she could see the pride in his dark eyes. "Great. He's a fast learner. I think he's a born woodworker like his dad. I'm having to relearn things myself just to keep up with him."

She took a sip of her coffee. "I watched you the other day. You're very good with him, very patient and encouraging."

"He's a good kid. I wish his dad could be here to see how well he's doing."

"I wish they could both be here for tomorrow."

Zach frowned, his dark brows narrowing. "Tomorrow?"

"Katie's birthday. We're having her party right after supper. I told you about this last week."

He leaned back in his chair. "Right. I remember now. Sorry, but I've had other things on my mind. Like getting this closet done and trying to find a job." He stood and went to the counter, dropping two pieces of bread into the toaster.

A knot formed in her chest. How could the man be so dense? "Do you know when DJ's birthday is?"

He hesitated while taking the butter from the fridge. "It's around one of the holidays."

"How about Linney?"

"That's easy. She was born the day after my birthday."

If he wanted to be a good father to these children, he should at least know when they were born. "Birthdays are important to children, Zach. It's a special day to them. Tomorrow Katie gets to be a princess all day. She said that's what her mom did every year. And I intend to continue the tradition."

He didn't comment as he buttered his toast.

She was beginning to wonder if he was a suitable guardian for her sister's children. One minute he was all devoted and committed, the next he didn't have a clue about anything.

She brushed off her irritation. "Don't forget to get a present."

"I'll pick something up while I'm in Memphis."

Sophie lowered her cup. "I thought you were going to Boise?"

"That got rescheduled. I'm flying a local businessman to check on his dealerships around the South."

"How long will you be gone?"

"Most of the day. We'll be going to Birmingham, Huntsville and Memphis."

A small knot of anxiety formed her chest. "You won't be late for the party, will you? Katie is looking forward to her family party."

"I shouldn't be."

Not the definitive response she'd been hoping for.

Just then, Katie walked into the kitchen. "Morning, Aunt Sophie." Katie hugged her around the waist. "Uncle Zach, tomorrow is my birthday party. We're going to have a special cake and everything. It's a book party." She gave him a hug, too.

"Sounds like fun. I should be home in plenty of time."

"Where are you going?"

"I have to fly some people around tomorrow."

"But you'll be at the party, won't you?"

"Sure."

"Promise?"

"I promise."

"Good. It won't be the same if you're not here." Katie smiled, then left the room.

Heat rose swiftly up through Sophie's throat. "I hope you meant that promise."

His dark eyes narrowed and his jaw tightened. "I'll keep it."

"I hope so because I don't want to see Katie's heart broken."

She rinsed her cup and walked out. She had work to do. With the remodeling back on track, she had to finalize the decor. She'd settled on the flooring but the countertops, hardware and paint colors were still undecided.

She would have to trust Zach would keep his word and be home in time for the party. If not, she would definitely give him a piece of her mind.

Zach took a seat in Hank's office early the next morning, leaned back and crossed his ankles. Sophie's stern words were still scratching against his mood like a bug bite. "Today is Katie's birthday and I promised to be at her party."

"Shouldn't be a problem. Mr. Habersham's three stops aren't that far apart so you won't be gone long. Besides, this guy is a good customer and he'll pay you a handsome bonus if he likes you."

It was a good opportunity and he needed every penny until a real job came through. Hank was his only source of income for the time being. Zach did a quick calculation in his head. Even allowing for longer meetings than planned, he'd be back before supper and in plenty of time for the party. An uneasy tightness settled in his chest. Sophie had made a big point of him being at this party. No, of him keeping his promise. It had been a command, really. A threat. As if he would suffer extreme consequences for failing to show up.

Surely she understood he wouldn't break a promise. Unless, of course, something more important turned up.

His conscience burned like a hot poker in his mind. That was the same rationalization he'd used when he'd told his brother he couldn't fly them home from their trip because he had to go to Dallas to test-fly a new helicopter design. It hadn't been a lie, but not exactly the truth either. It was something he'd wanted to do. An opportunity he hadn't wanted to pass up. So, he'd broken his promise. And Dean and Maddie had died.

Sometimes being around Sophie left him edgy and confused and he didn't like the feeling. She puzzled him and intrigued him at the same time. She also made him feel as if she could see right through him to who he was and found him lacking. No one had ever made him feel like that before. She always forced him to take a closer look at himself.

He tapped his fingers on the arm of the chair. "Do you know the birthdays of your nieces and nephews?"

Hank stared at him a long moment. "I have seven of them. No, not all of them. Why?"

Zach rubbed his forehead. "Today is Katie's birthday."

"Ah. And you didn't remember. Well, it's not too late to pick up a gift."

"That's not the problem. Sophie gave me a lecture on how important it is to keep promises to kids."

Hank nodded in agreement. "It is. That's why I'm very careful when I promise something to my boys."

"Have you ever broken one?"

"A few times. It wasn't pretty. I felt really bad and I had to deal with a disappointed son for a long while. Not to mention a wife who was ready to send me to the doghouse permanently."

"But they got over it, right? I mean, it couldn't be helped."

"Yes, and you're right. It couldn't have been helped, but to a five-year-old that doesn't mean anything. All they know is that their dad was supposed to be somewhere and he didn't show up. After that, it's hard to regain their trust."

Broken promises. Zach was all too aware of the consequences. But he hadn't equated that to making a promise to his niece. "I guess I have a lot to learn about being a parent."

Hank chuckled softly. "You are taking a crash course, my friend. Don't be so hard on yourself. But you might want to put the kids' birthdays in your phone and make a reminder for yourself."

"Yeah. Great idea. I'll do that." Gathering up his gear, Zach went out to the plane and started his pre-flight check. He had to backtrack a few times when his concern about the promise thing took over his thoughts.

Thankfully, his passenger arrived and he was able to shove his concern into a back corner of his mind, but not before making a promise to himself to be back home in plenty of time for Katie's party tonight no matter what.

By four o'clock that afternoon, Zach's promise to himself was starting to look like a no-go. His passenger had added two more stops to their flight plan. One in Little Rock and another in Mobile. Each stop so far had taken an hour or more longer than the man had estimated. Zach did a quick calculation. If they kept to a good schedule, he'd be home in the nick of time. If anything went wrong, he'd be in hot water.

Thankfully he'd picked up a gift along the way and had it wrapped so he was good on that front. He sent up a prayer for smooth sailing as his passenger came toward him over the tarmac. So far this stop had gone as planned. Only one more to go.

Mr. Habersham was an hour late returning to the FBO in Mobile and Zach was getting antsy. Bad weather threatened. If they could get in the air soon, he could fly around it but it would play havoc with his timetable.

He finished his preflight check and prepared to taxi. He couldn't worry about broken promises now. He needed all his skill and concentration to get them home safely and pray his family would understand and that little Katie would forgive him.

And that Sophie wouldn't throttle him.

Sophie checked the clock again, gritting her teeth. If she could get her hands on Zack right now, she would cheerfully wring his stubborn, clueless neck. It was well past supper time and there was no sign of him. He hadn't even bothered to call. She'd managed to persuade Katie to eat, reminding her that Zach had promised to be there and that sometimes planes ran late. But that wasn't going to satisfy her much longer. Even Linney was getting agitated.

She'd called Zach's cell but it went to voice mail. She'd phoned Hank but he wasn't aware of any problems. He promised to call if he heard anything. An hour later he'd called to explain about the additional stops the passenger had added and the bad weather.

Katie's irritation level rose steadily with each passing minute. The children were getting anxious. What worried her was that they weren't upset about the party, but that something might have happened to their uncle. She had to admit she was also becoming concerned. Zach may have a lot to learn about parenting, but she knew he wouldn't deliberately miss the party without some reasonable explanation.

Her throat seized up. That left another frightening

possibility. What if something *had* happened to him and he couldn't call? Her concern spiked to alarm when Linney burst into the room sobbing.

"He's dead. Uncle Zach is dead like Mommy and Daddy."

Her heart chilled. Sophie picked her up and held her close. "Oh, no, Linney. I'm sure he's fine. He's just running late. Hank said the man he was flying around added a few more stops to the trip. That's all." She decided not to mention the weather. "It'll be all right, sweetheart. He'll be here soon and we'll have Katie's party just like we planned."

Linney shook her head against Sophie's neck. "No. He's dead. Everyone said Mommy and Daddy were late, too. Only they weren't. They never came home. They went to heaven instead. I don't want Uncle Zach to go to heaven."

Sophie didn't know how to comfort the little girl. She clutched the child closer, making soothing sounds and praying for something reassuring to say.

Katie approached, her eyes wet with tears. "Uncle Zach isn't coming home is he? His plane crashed. Like Mom and Dad's car. That's why he's late, huh?"

"No. I'm sure that's not it. He's just late."

"We know when grown-ups are lying."

DJ leaned against the doorjamb. "They kept telling us our parents were coming home, but they never did."

Sophie wanted desperately to give them words of hope, but she was beginning to feel the fear herself. Katie started to sob, and Sophie ushered them into the living room, gathering them on the sofa and trying to comfort them the best she knew how.

"Let's say a prayer for his safe return and that he'll be home soon."

They prayed, but it did nothing to calm them. Linney had worked herself up into a crying jag that shook her little body. "What will we do without Uncle Zach? Who will take care of us?"

"We'll go to foster care, that's what. They'll send us to live with mean people."

Sophie scowled. "DJ. Stop talking like that. You're scaring your sisters. Nothing has happened to your uncle. Besides, you have me now. Everything is going to be all right."

"You won't go anywhere, will you? You'll stay here forever?" Katie looked up at her with pleading eyes.

If only Sophie could make that promise. "Hush. Don't worry. I'm here." She stroked Katie's hair, praying that she could always be a part of their lives.

The sound of the back door opening woke her. Linney was asleep with her head in Sophie's lap. Katie was curled up beside her on the sofa. DJ was laid back in the recliner deep in sleep.

Zach stepped into the family room, sending a torrent of mixed emotions through her veins. Relief that he was home safe, and fury that he'd put them through this trauma without any thought of them.

She avoided looking at him, turning her attention to the girls and gently stirring them awake. "Uncle Zach is home safe and sound."

Linney rubbed her eyes, took one look at her uncle and screeched. She flew off the sofa and charged toward him. "I thought you were dead."

Zach was clearly shocked at her words as he picked her up and held her close. "I'm fine, Linney Bug. It's okay."

Katie woke next and ran to her uncle. "Don't go to heaven, Uncle Zach, please don't go there. Where were you? We thought you'd died. Why didn't you call us?"

The little girl had voiced all of Sophie's concerns, so she stood and watched as DJ rose from the recliner. "Not cool, Uncle Zach. Not cool." He headed up the stairs.

Sophie faced the man, arms crossed over her chest. The girls were still crying, Zach's reassurances having little effect. He looked lost and confused but she didn't offer to help. Let the man figure out how to appease them.

Linney finally stopped crying and Katie eased her grip around his waist.

Sophie took the opportunity to steer them off to bed.

"What about my party?" Katie asked.

Sophie had long ago put the cake back in the refrigerator and cleared away the birthday paper plates. "We'll celebrate tomorrow."

Linney took Sophie's hand but stopped and looked back at Zach. "Will you be here in the morning?"

"Yes, of course. I promise."

Katie frowned. "You promised to be here for the party, too. But you weren't."

Sophie shot a glare in his direction, then guided the girls up to bed. It took her a while to get them settled down, and when she went back downstairs, Zach was nowhere to be found.

She finally tracked him to the front porch sitting in one of the rockers. She sat in the other one, struggling to find the words. She couldn't decide whether to be gracious and hear his side of the story or launch into her tirade about breaking promises.

She chose to wait for him to initiate the conversation.

Chapter Seven

Zach tensed when Sophie came out onto the porch. She sat in the other rocker, stiff, disapproving, exuding anger. He tried his best to wait for her scolding, but she remained silent and unmoving. After a long silence, he began to squirm. He'd been in this position before as a kid waiting for his father to punish him for something he'd done. He might as well face the music because Sophie was obviously going to make him *fess up*, as his dad used to say.

He took a deep breath and prayed for courage. "I didn't mean to break my promise. It couldn't be helped."

She didn't answer right away but when she spoke her tone was icy cold. "Which is why you shouldn't make promises unless you are certain you can keep them."

He looked at her but she was staring straight ahead. "That's an impossible request to make of anyone."

"No, it's not. It's simple. Just don't make promises. Or you could call and let others know you're running late."

"I can't use a cell phone when I'm flying."

"What about between flights?"

Zach exhaled a deep sigh. "It was a very hectic day. The passenger added two more cities to the itinerary. I'm lucky I even had time to get Katie a gift."

"It would have been better if you'd been here."

"I didn't know they'd be so upset."

She finally faced him. "You heard them, Zach. They thought you were dead. Linney was hysterical at one point. It was all I could do to calm her down. Katie cried and prayed over and over that you wouldn't go to heaven."

Bile rose in his throat and a knot formed inside his rib cage. "I never intended for this to happen. I had no idea they'd react that way."

"You should have. They've lost their parents. Of course they'd think the worst when the only person left to them didn't come home. They were reliving that day, Zach. Surely you can understand that."

He did. And she was right. He should have foreseen this kind of reaction. Another mega failure as a parent. Would he ever get the hang of raising his family? "So how do I fix this?"

"You don't fix this Zach. The damage has been done. You broke your promise. Now you have to work on re-building their trust."

Zach looked at her. "What is it with you and promises? My parents made promises that sometimes they couldn't keep. We were supposed to go on a beach trip one summer, but my dad lost a contracting job at the last minute and we couldn't go. We were disappointed but it didn't scar us for life."

He met Sophie's gaze; her eyes widened and she

clasped her hands together. Even in the dim porch light he could see how pale she'd become. He sensed there was something deeper to her passion about promises. "Who broke a promise to you, Sophie, that you're so fierce about keeping them?"

She turned away, her head bowed. He reached out to her, then thought better of the idea. It might be best to not force the issue.

"Everyone."

She spoke the word so softly he wasn't sure he'd heard it. His heart ached. What had happened to her? Slowly he extended his hand and lightly touched her forearm. She winced and pulled away.

"Who, Sophie?"

He watched her spine stiffen, her head lift, and she turned to face him, her lips in a hard line. "My sister promised we'd stay together no matter what, but she walked out in the middle of the night and disappeared. My father promised to take care of me, that I'd never be alone, but he dumped me at my aunt's two weeks after my mother died. My fiancé promised to love me forever, until he found someone better."

His heart sank. "Those are big promises to break."

"You may not have scars from your broken promises but I do. They changed my life. If they hadn't promised, then it wouldn't have hurt so much. There are tragic consequences to breaking a promise."

If she'd jammed a knife into his chest, it couldn't have hurt more. His mouth filled with a metallic taste. He knew only too well the consequences of breaking a promise. He lived them every time he looked at the kids.

"I'll talk to the kids tomorrow and assure them that

it won't happen again. But I won't promise anything."
He hoped his light tone would ease her tension, but she
kept her face averted. A light breeze stirred her hair and
she brushed it aside. It struck him that as much as she
resembled her sister physically, she was really a different person. "You're nothing like your sister."

Her soft inhale of breath told him he'd said the exact
wrong thing.

"I'm very aware of that. Maddie was the pretty one,
the smart one, the bubbly one, the one that drew everyone to her and made them feel special. I was the shy
mouse hiding in the corner."

"I just meant that—"

She held up her hand. "You just wish I'd be more like
my sister. Well, I'm *not* her and I can't ever be like her."

She went inside, letting the door slam behind her.

Zach rested his head on the back of the rocker, grip-
ping the wooded arms in his hands. He should have
known better than to try to talk about this situation.
He was lousy at talking. He always said the wrong
thing. Talking only led to more trouble and more mis-
understanding.

He had to make this right but he had no idea how to
go about it. Life was so much simpler when he only had
to worry about himself. He wasn't cut out for being a
dad, a parent, holding a family together. *Lord, why have
You put me here? I can't take the place of their parents.*
Sophie made a better guardian than he could ever be.
Maybe it would be best for everyone if she took over.
But how would he survive without the kids? They were
a part of him now. His family.

Zach slowly rose from the rocker and headed inside.

There was nothing he could do tonight. He'd tackle everything tomorrow. There were several closet projects that would be finished and then he could turn things over to Sophie for the finishing touches.

Zach's toast popped up just as Linney grabbed his leg and hugged it tight. He smiled and rested a hand on her head. "Good morning."

She looked up at him with big blue eyes "I was afraid you wouldn't be here."

He winced. He'd hoped last night would be forgotten in the light of day but apparently not. "I'm here, Linney Bug, and I'm not going anywhere."

"Good. I'm hungry."

Zach fixed a bowl of cereal and set it in front of her, joining her at the table and taking a bite of his toast. He searched around for words to explain about last night. Sophie's words still rang in his head. He'd grossly underestimated the effect being late would have on the kids.

"I'm sorry about Katie's party last night. I was looking forward to it."

"That's okay. I was just scared. Mommy and Daddy didn't come home, and I was afraid you wouldn't either. DJ said we'd have to go live with mean people in frosty care."

The bite of toast lodged in Zach's throat. "I'd never let that happen. I'll always be here for you and your brother and sister. Besides, you have Aunt Sophie now, too. She loves you."

Linney smiled. "I love her, too. It's almost like having Mommy here."

Zach kissed her forehead. "She's very nice."

"Hey, Uncle Zach." Katie came to his side and wrapped her arms around his neck, squeezing tightly. "I'm so glad you're home. I was really, *really* worried."

He rested his hand on her arm, aware of how small and vulnerable she was. Sophie was right, he didn't really understand what the kids needed. But he was beginning to. They needed more of him. He just didn't know how he would do that. He still needed a full-time job, but flying charters for Hank and being a flight instructor weren't enough.

Maybe he could start by trying to make up for last night. "Katie, how about we have your party now?"

She stared at him, wide-eyed. "You mean at breakfast time?"

"Why not?"

"I think that's a good idea."

Zach looked over his shoulder as Sophie entered the kitchen. "Instead of a party after supper, we'll have it after breakfast. The cake is still in the fridge. All we have to do is cut it and dish up the ice cream."

Linney raised her hand. "Don't forget the gummy worms on top."

"Not a chance," Sophie said. "Katie, go wake your brother. Linney, please bring the presents from the family room and put them on the counter. Uncle Zach and I will get everything ready."

Zach carried his cup and plate to the sink avoiding Sophie's gaze. How much had she heard? Was she trying to help him save face or was she attempting to keep his guilt alive? He wished he could read her better, he was always doubting her sincerity. Could anyone really be as caring and considerate as Sophie Armstrong?

Sophie instructed him as he went about the preparations silently. She seemed relaxed and friendly this morning but how would he know? Only one way to find out.

"Sophie, I'm sorry, I shouldn't have compared you to Maddie last night. I didn't mean it the way it sounded."

She froze for a moment, then finished slicing the cake. "Don't worry about it."

What did that mean? Was she saying it really hadn't bothered her or that it had but she wasn't going to discuss it? He placed the pitcher of lemonade on the table. "I want you to know, I meant it in a good way. That you're not like Maddie, I mean."

She faced him, a frown marring her forehead. "I thought you liked my sister."

"I did. But she was always moving, always busy, always rushing off to the next project. Being around her could be exhausting."

"As opposed to me, who fades quietly into the background. I've heard it all before."

Zach faced her. "No. Why do you do that?"

"Do what?"

"Put yourself down whenever anyone tries to compliment you."

"I don't do that."

He nodded. "You do."

She inhaled a slow breath as if trying to measure her response. "I know I'm nothing like my sister. My mother always told me, my teachers told me, my friends told me. Even my first employer suggested I join Toastmasters to gain a little more self-confidence. I'm just not made that way. I like things quiet and orderly. I like to take my time with things."

"I *like* that you're that way. You're peaceful."

She scowled. Had he blundered again?

"You've brought a quiet contentment to this house," he insisted. "I can see it in the kids. They're sleeping better and eating better. It's like they took a deep breath after you came. As if they knew they were safe now and everything was going to be all right."

A slow smile appeared on her lips and kindled a light in her eyes. He'd never realized how pretty she was. Not the flashy kind like her sister, but a soft, subtle, timeless beauty. His heart started thudding in his chest.

"Thank you. That's one of the nicest things anyone has said to me. Most people are put off by my shyness. But I usually prefer spending time alone to going to parties and get-togethers. All that small talk and chatter make me tired." She handed him the bowl of gummy worms. "I think we're ready for the party."

He took the bowl, their fingers touching. A warmth spread through him. "I'm sorry about last night. Being late and not calling. I never imagined the kids would be so upset."

"You're their world now, Zach. They love you. You have to think of that when you're dealing with them."

"I get that now. But the kids love you, too."

She chuckled softly and looked away. "That's just because I talked you into doing the closet project."

Before he could correct her statement, Katie rushed in with a happy Linney on her heels and a very drowsy DJ bringing up the rear.

"Is the party ready?"

"All set. Katie, you take the seat of honor." Sophie had tied a large purple bow to the back of one chair. "And here is your princess crown for the day." She placed a glittery plastic tiara on her head.

Zach presented her with the first piece of cake and bowl of ice cream, chuckling as she piled gummy worms on top. He took a seat, giving himself over to the party and counting his blessings. He loved these kids. He loved having his own family and he loved that Sophie had knocked on his door and become one of them. She smiled over the table at him as Katie started opening her gifts, and he realized that his feelings for the surprise aunt had changed. He liked her. He more than liked her. He was interested in her. It was a sobering thought and one he wasn't quite sure he wanted to pursue. He diverted his thoughts by handing his niece another gift.

He wasn't cut out for being a husband any more than he was a father. But somehow, Sophie made him want to learn.

Sophie strolled through the old bus station, excitement swelling in her heart as she took in the progress. Zach and the volunteers had done wonders in only four weeks. It might look like a historic bus station on the outside, but inside it was a neat charity closet just waiting for inventory to fill the space. There were a few things still to do but she could start moving clothing into the store in a matter of days.

She rubbed her fingertips over her chin. What would Maddie think of the result? Was it what she had envisioned? There had been some adjustments made to her sister's plan but nothing major. Overall, the shop looked nice, welcoming but not overly decorated. A simple place where those in need could find the assistance they needed to make a new start without any judgment or sense of shame.

The store was empty of helpers today. Zach had assured her it was a temporary lull. Work would pick up in the afternoon. The silence was a welcome change. It gave her time to soak in the progress and plan her next decision.

Pulling out her sketch pad, she flipped through the pages, stopping on the one she'd done during Katie's party. Zach had a big smile on his face and love for his kids was shining brightly in his dark eyes. Katie hugged the collection of books he'd given her, and Linney, close at his side, looked up at him with adoration. DJ, ever the cool dude, leaned elbows on the table with a half smile.

Her family. Sophie's heart felt warmed with love.

The party had been the first time since she'd arrived at the Conrad house when she'd truly felt as if she was part of it all. They'd laughed and joked and enjoyed cake and ice cream for breakfast. The fear and disappointment of the previous night had been forgotten, replaced with happy memories.

Turning to a blank page, Sophie scanned the area where the clothing racks would stand, picturing how it would all play out. She sketched the vision in her mind, pleased with the final image.

She started when she heard footsteps behind her. She quickly turned the page back. "Oh."

Zach held up a hand. "Sorry, I thought you heard me come in."

She shook her head. "No problem. I tend to zone out when I'm sketching."

He looked over her shoulder. "It's the party. Katie sure looks happy."

"I know. It was everything she'd hoped her party would be. That was a good idea you had, Zach. You were the hero this morning."

He shifted his weight as if uncomfortable with her compliment. "Drawing helps you think?"

"It helps a lot of things." She laid the book on the corner of the desk and looked up at him. "What brings you here? I thought you were giving flying lessons this morning."

"The student canceled. I picked up the light fixtures for the bathrooms and the fitting rooms. I take it the kids got off all right this morning?"

"They were excited about going to Biloxi with Rachel and her family for a day at the beach."

"I'm sure." He held her gaze a moment as if wanting to say more before grinning and moving away. "I'd better get these fixtures installed."

Sophie released a breath she didn't realize she'd been holding. She did that often when Zach was close. Odd. His nearness triggered a confusing, nervous, edgy warmth and a sharp wariness as if he was dangerous. Silly. There was nothing dangerous about Zach. It was very strange. But then, he was a puzzling man. She never could predict his reactions to things. Maybe in time she would, though time was running out. In two weeks she'd have to decide if she was going back to

Ohio or staying in Mississippi. That decision depended on Zach.

"Look who stopped by to check on the closet." Zach strolled into the office, arms full of boxes, with a tall, robust black man in a sport coat right behind him. She recognized him as Isaac Drummond, long-time mayor of Blessing.

"Good morning, Miss Armstrong. Looks like you're nearly ready for business."

"Yes, sir. We'll start bringing in the clothes early next week."

"Marvelous. I wanted to talk to you about this building but I see now it might be too late. Is there any way this structure could be declared a historic landmark? One of the council members suggested it to me."

Sophie glanced at Zach. "I'm afraid not. My sister looked into that and the building has been remodeled too many times to qualify. However we do intend to keep the outside as true to the era as possible."

Drummond smiled. "Good to hear. With the bicentennial coming up, we want to showcase our historic architecture and our service organizations as much as possible." His gaze landed on the sketchbook she'd laid on the counter, still open to the family drawing. He leaned over for a better look. "Did you do these?"

"Yes. Just a hobby of mine."

"You're quite talented. You should enter the poster contest."

"Poster contest?"

"For the official bicentennial poster. It'll be on all our marketing materials, including T-shirts. There's a sizeable cash prize for the winner."

The idea appealed to her. She normally avoided sharing her drawings with anyone, but the idea of being part of Blessing's upcoming celebration made her feel like part of the community. "Oh, I don't know. I'll think about it."

"Wonderful. Well, I'll let you get on with the work." He shook hands with them then walked out.

Zach grinned, nodding toward her sketchbook. "I think the mayor's right. You should go for it, Sophie. You're very talented."

His encouragement made her smile. "I won a prize in school once for my drawing. The only thing I ever won." She'd been seven, and when she'd shown her mother the ribbon, she'd laughed at her and said it must have been a mistake.

"See there. It's a sign you should try again."

A loud clap of thunder rattled the windows. Sophie jumped, her hand at her throat, heart pounding.

"Looks like that thunderstorm they predicted is rolling in. Maybe we should close up and head home." Before Zach could blink, the sky opened up and rain poured down in sheets. "Or we could stay here."

Sophie stepped to the window, watching the lightning flash in the sky. "I hope it doesn't last long." A churning sensation started in her stomach.

"It won't. It's just a summer storm. Don't you like storms?"

"I do, usually. Maddie and I used to sit on the front porch when it rained and read or play games." Another boom shattered the air, followed by a loud crack, and the store went dark.

"Well, I suppose we might as well wait it out in here,"

Zach said. "At least there's a window for light and we can open it a crack for some air. With no AC, it'll get stuffy in here soon."

He pulled up another folding chair to the gate-leg table that was serving as a temporary desk until the permanent one could be installed. "I think there're some drinks and cookies in the break room."

She shook her head. "I'm good."

"Okay, be right back."

When he returned, he was carrying two bottles of water and a small box of cookies. His gaze fell on her sketchbook. She reached for the book but he picked it up, turning it so she could see the image. The family party. She looked away.

"This is very good. I feel like I'm there again. But there's one thing missing."

"What?"

"You." He handed the sketchbook to her. "The picture's not complete without you, Sophie. That whole party was your idea. It was the perfect day for Katie."

"I hope so. I know it was hard for her not having her mom and dad here this year."

"You'll make a great mother someday."

If he'd stabbed her with a knife, it couldn't have hurt more. "No. I won't." She shoved the sketchbook aside and turned away.

"Of course you will. You'll meet a guy and settle down and have kids of your own."

She shook her head, fighting back tears. "No. That'll never happen for me."

"Why not?"

No point in hiding the truth. "I had an infection that

required surgery. I'll never have children of my own. Maddie's children are the only family I'll ever have."

Zach set his hands on his hips and glanced at the ceiling briefly. "Oh, Sophie. That's rough. I don't know what to say."

She forced a smile. "Nothing to say. It is what it is."

"But you were made to be a mother. I mean, you're so good with kids. I'm sure you'll find someone who won't care about that."

"I think the Lord wants me to be alone." She exhaled a sardonic huff. "Even my engagement fell through. He said I wasn't smart enough for him."

"That's ridiculous. You're one of the smartest people I know. Look what you've done here at the store. You took Maddie's ideas and notes and made it all a reality."

"That wasn't me. That was all my sister. I just followed her plan. She was the smart one. Straight A's, honor society. I had to study twice as hard just to get by. I was never book smart like her. Or you. I'll bet you aced every class."

He shrugged. "I guess. But you have people smarts, and that's something I don't have. Dean had that in spades, like you. He had a way of making people feel relaxed as if they'd been friends forever. I usually avoid people. I'm happier when I'm alone."

"Like when you're alone in the sky."

"Yeah. No secret there. My ex broke up with me because she said I wasn't good husband material. I didn't know how to connect with people. She wasn't entirely wrong. I think I avoided my family because they didn't understand my passion for flying. I was different from them so I just went my own way."

She traced a raindrop as it slid down the outside of the pane. "Maybe that's what Maddie did. Went her own way."

A lightning strike and a boom of thunder sent Sophie backing away from the window and into Zach's solid chest. His hands gently gripped her shoulders. Her mind told her to move away, but her body refused to comply. Zach slowly turned her around. She kept her eyes lowered, afraid of what she might see in his dark gaze. Or what she wouldn't.

"It's only light and noise, Sophie. Nothing to be afraid of."

She looked up into his eyes. Her heart raced. He was wrong. There was a great deal to be afraid of. Their eyes locked. She held her breath, unwilling to spoil the moment. But then he looked away, dropped his hands and stepped back.

Just as quickly as it had started, the storm ended. The power blinked on and the shop filled with the sounds of the AC kicking on and the fridge in the break room stirring to life.

Heat crawled up Sophie's neck. She slipped past Zach, gathered her belongings and started for the door. "I'd better get home."

"Right. I'll finish up here first. We're running out of time. You'll be leaving soon."

She stopped, her throat tightening. There it was. His subtle reminder that she wasn't wanted here. Unable to stop herself, she turned and looked at him over her shoulder. There was a small grin on his face but his brown eyes said something else. She just didn't understand what.

There was no point in saying anything. She walked out, determined not to cry until she was alone.

Maddie had always accused her of having fanciful ideas. She'd proved it with Zach just now. For a moment she'd thought she'd seen affection in his eyes. She'd allowed herself to believe that he'd felt that between them.

But it was nothing more than her fanciful thinking.

Zach watched Sophie walk out of the store, mentally kicking himself for his stupidity. He'd upset her again. How he wasn't sure, but he had. It always went like this when he tried to talk to people about important things. He mucked it all up.

He walked to the window, resting his forearm high on the frame, and watched as her car pulled away, scattering water as she went. The same way she scattered his thoughts.

He'd wanted to comfort her. Learning she couldn't have children had stung him to the core. Why would that happen to a woman like her? Someone so kind, so loving and so perfect for motherhood? It was a shame.

He turned away. He should get back to work. How was he supposed to concentrate on light fixtures when he was hurting for his friend? No. Somewhere along the way, she'd gone from relative to friend to more. He cared for her deeply. The realization sent a shard of ice through his veins. It was a new sensation. An emotion he'd never attached to a woman before.

She stirred a lot of strange emotions. Most he couldn't even name, but he always felt oddly cut off, adrift when she wasn't around. Holding her close had set off a whirlwind of feelings so quick and intense he'd been unable to process them. He'd looked into her eyes and the world had shifted in a direction he'd never known. He'd wanted to draw her closer and kiss her.

But instead he'd backed away, not sure what to do with his feelings. He wasn't sure what he'd said after that. He'd babbled some platitudes but his words had clearly upset her.

He huffed out a low grunt. Women. Who could figure them out?

"Hey there, Zach old boy."

"Hank. What brings you by?" His friend's unexpected appearance was like a blessed reprieve from his thoughts.

"I wanted to see if there was anything I could do around here. I've got some free time so I'm available. And also, there's a charter schedule for tomorrow. It's a quick up-and-back I thought you might like to take. It's a bit unusual but I'll explain that later."

"Okay. Sounds interesting. I'm ready for a break from all this ground work. You want a drink?"

"Sure." Hank wandered through the old building before rejoining Zach in the breakroom. He was carrying Sophie's sketch pad when he returned. "Whose is this?"

"Oh. That's Sophie's. She must have forgotten it when she left." The book was open to the birthday drawing.

"She's very good."

Zach nodded. "The mayor invited her to enter the bicentennial poster contest."

"She could win. She captured the family perfectly."

"You think so? I mean, the kids are good but that doesn't look anything like me."

Hank took another look at the sketch and chuckled. "It looks exactly like you."

Zach made a dismissive gesture. "Aw, come on. My jaw isn't that sharp and I never have a cocky smirk on my face. Why would she draw me that way?"

Hank leaned in and tapped the sketch with one finger. "You really are clueless, aren't you? She probably drew this with her heart."

"Meaning?"

"Figure it out, pal." Hank chuckled and waved him forward. "Let's get those fixtures installed."

Zach studied the sketch several more times after Hank left. Whatever his friend was trying to tell him was lost on him. The kids were drawn to perfection, but why would Sophie draw him like a handsome hero? It made no sense. He'd done little heroic since her arrival. To be truthful, he'd acted anything but heroic.

"Hello? Anyone here?"

Zach hurried to the front of the store. He recognized that voice. It was Alice Smiley, the heart of the Blessing Community Church. "Miss Alice. So nice to see you. What can I do for you?"

"Well, I wanted to see the progress but I was hoping Sophie would be here. At eighty-five years young, I can't do much to help with the remodel, but I can surely hang and tag clothes."

"I'm sure Sophie would be grateful for your help."

"It's a wonderful thing she's done here. All of you. What a shame Madeline couldn't see it all come together."

Zach could only nod. Words wouldn't come through his tight throat.

"Well, I won't keep you. I'll call Sophie. Do you have her cell number?"

"Yes." Alice handed him her phone, and he punched in the number. When he handed it back, Alice was looking at the family sketch.

"Very nice." She grinned and winked. "Whoever drew this has a big crush on you, young man." She slipped her phone into her purse and waved goodbye.

Zach studied the drawing again. What was it that everyone saw but him? Sophie was talented. More than he'd realized. Her sketch of the birthday party was amazing. She'd captured every kid perfectly, each little nuance and quirk. She'd been more than flattering to him, giving him a square jawline, eyes filled with joy and a crooked smile that made him look like a rascal.

The image of him was far too handsome and attractive. It was like she'd drawn him the way she'd like him to be or the way she saw him. Could that be what Hank meant when he said she'd drawn him with her heart? Did Sophie see him like this? Kind, heroic, appealing? He was none of those things. He was just a thirty-three-year-old single guy trying to make sense of his new world and failing miserably.

However, it did beg the question, did she have feelings for him?

His thoughts drifted to the moment she'd backed into him and he'd held her close. Was that what he'd seen in her eyes? What had scared him off? If she did have feelings for him and he for her, what happened next?

No. It was too ridiculous. Sophie only cared for the kids. It was all about the nieces and nephew. Nothing more.

So why did he want it to be more?

Chapter Eight

Sophie stretched her fingers, working out the cramps from holding her drawing pencil so long. She hadn't seriously considered entering the poster contest, but then she heard her aunt's voice in her head urging her to try something new. She needed a distraction, some time in her safe zone.

Her mind was so cluttered with confusion and doubt, it was difficult to think clearly. The closet project kept her occupied during the day. There were so many details to attend to now that the building was almost ready. The evenings were filled with the children and Zach. Her most confusing issue. Then when she went to her room at night, her thoughts turned to Maddie and all those missing years and the reasons behind them. Working on the poster kept her mind occupied.

She was pleased with the rough sketch she'd done for it. She'd tried to incorporate all the things she'd come to love about Blessing, starting with the Blessing Bridge. She'd placed it in the center, then added the white steeple on the historic church and the courthouse clock tower. Next she'd included a section of the ruins of Afton Grove Plantation, visible through the trees at the bridge. Finally she sketched a collection of Main Street stores and the pathway in Riverbank Park that hugged the scenic Silver River.

The more time she'd spent exploring the town, the more she'd fallen in love with her temporary home. It was the kind of small town everyone dreamed of living in, and a far cry from the hustle and bustle of Columbus, Ohio. It would be so easy to live here. She could understand why Maddie had been so happy here.

Sophie glanced around the master bedroom. Had Maddie been so happy here that she'd forgotten all about her younger sister? Why would she let everyone think she had no family? Mostly, Sophie wanted to know why Maddie had walked away from her family fifteen years ago and never returned.

Forcing those questions aside, she turned her focus to the sketch. Tomorrow she'd visit the local art shop she'd seen in town and pick up watercolor supplies to finish the poster. The deadline was looming and she was determined to enter.

Setting aside her drawing, she headed to the bathroom to prepare for bed.

Linney's shrill screams froze her in place. The girls' room was right above the master. Heart pounding, she hurried from her room and up the stairs.

DJ was leaning against the doorjamb of Linney and Katie's room as she approached. He glanced over his shoulder. "Linney had another nightmare." His tone was sour but his eyes said something else entirely. He was worried about his sister and probably grieving himself.

Sophie stepped in the doorway and looked in. Linney's sobs were heartrending.

Zach was already sitting on the bed, holding Linney in his lap, rocking back and forth in a comforting manner. The little girl clutched his shirt in her fist.

"I want them back. Why can't they come back?"

"I want them back, too, sweetie. I miss them."

Katie scooted out of her bed and joined her uncle. "I miss them, too, but they're really happy in heaven with Jesus."

"I want them happy here with us."

Katie's attempt at comfort only resulted in more sobs. Sophie kept out of sight, not wanting to intrude on the moment. Zach had the situation under control and was doing a good job. The girls obviously drew comfort from their uncle. They loved him and he loved them deeply.

Linney had finally stopped crying. "You won't go anywhere, will you, Uncle Zach?"

"I'll be right here to take care of you and your brother and sister. I promise."

Sophie winced. She couldn't help but worry about that, especially if he insisted on a flying career.

Katie patted her sister's shoulder. "You can sleep with me if you want to."

"Okay." Linney nodded, clutching her bear to her chest as she crawled into Katie's bed. Zach covered them both up with the blanket, kissed them and told them he loved them.

Sophie moved away down the hall, her heart aching for the children. She knew what it was like to lose her parents. But she'd been a teenager when it happened, and had understood the concept of death. These little girls were too young to comprehend.

"Sophie."

She stopped when Zach called her name and slowly turned to face him.

"I didn't know you were there. Did you hear Linney?"

"I heard her scream, but when I got up here, you were already with her." She looked into his eyes, still filled with sadness for their nieces. "You were wonderful with Linney. Does she get like this very often?"

"Not so much anymore."

"They love you very much. I just wish…that you hadn't promised to never go away. You can't promise that. None of us can."

"It's what she needed to hear. And I'm not going anywhere. The Lord wouldn't take me away, too, and leave them with no one." He held her gaze a moment. Then went down the hall to his room.

Sophie made her way back downstairs to the master bedroom and crawled under the covers. If she'd harbored any lingering doubts about Zach's devotion to their nieces and nephew, they had been banished tonight. They belonged together. While she was uncomfortable with his careless promise to them, she had to face the truth of the matter. He was the perfect person to be their guardian.

Secretly she'd held the belief that she was more qualified than Zach to raise the children. But after tonight, maybe she should learn to be content as the aunt who visited a couple times a year.

Tears stung her eyes and she slid deeper under the

covers. How could she be satisfied with only seeing them now and again when all she wanted was to be with them every minute?

Zach slipped his phone into his pocket, smiling. Hank had lined up a very special charter for today, something unusual and definitely not his normal passenger. He appreciated the quick turnaround since the charity closet was nearing completion and he had a list of details to take care of. DJ had become his welcome shadow and Zach thoroughly enjoyed teaching his nephew carpentry. He'd even started to enjoy working with his hands again. Nothing would take the place of flying, but he'd been surprised at the sense of satisfaction he'd gained from woodworking and the remodel.

The look of joy on Sophie's face each time he completed a cabinet or finished a construction project filled him with a sense of accomplishment and pleasure. He realized he liked making her happy.

He strolled into the kitchen where the kids were eating breakfast. "Morning, everyone. What big plans do y'all have for today?"

Sophie poured herself a glass of juice, then sat down at the table. "I have a long list of phone calls to make."

DJ glanced up. "I'm going to help Mr. Buck repair the damaged bricks on the outside of the store."

Sophie smiled and nodded. "The girls are going to paint the fitting rooms. They're very excited."

He could well imagine. He smiled at the mental picture of them slopping paint all over the place. "Who do you have in charge of clean up and repainting?"

"I get to use a little roller like the big ones the grown-ups use," Linney declared between bites of toast.

Katie looked at her uncle. "What are you going to do today, Uncle Zach?"

Sophie turned her smile on him and his heart did a funny jump inside his chest. Her smile was more brilliant than her sister's. It always made him feel as if someone had turned a light on inside of him. He cleared his throat and gathered his thoughts. "I've got a charter flight to New Orleans today."

The warmth in Sophie's eyes dimmed. "Will you be gone long?"

"No. It's a down-and-back. No layover."

"Are you going away again?"

The tension in Linney's voice concerned him. "Just for a few hours."

Her lower lip began to wobble and her eyes grew moist. "No. You can't. I don't want you to go! You have to stay here!"

He exchanged glances with Sophie. "I have to go, sweetie. It's my job."

"Nooo!" The word came out as a long wail. "What if you don't come back?"

"I'll come back. Honest." He almost added, *Promise*, but caught the warning in Sophie's eyes. "It's a quick trip. Nothing to worry about."

"But Mommy and Daddy didn't come home."

Zach's heart shredded. "I know, but I'm a really good pilot. The very best, so there's nothing to worry about." He had supreme confidence in his abilities, but that didn't prevent his mind from conjuring up all kinds of things that could go wrong, even with a skilled pilot.

Sophie put her arms around the little girl. "Don't worry, Linney. Uncle Zach will be very careful. Maybe he could call you from New Orleans and let you know he arrived safely."

Zach nodded, thankful for her idea. "I'll do that. Then you won't have to worry."

"No. You need to stay home. Please. I don't want you to go!"

Zach lifted her into his arms as her sobs increased. "It's all right, sweetie. Don't worry." He carried her into the family room and sat on the sofa, trying his best to comfort the little one. He couldn't find words so he simply held her and let her cry. Finally she calmed down.

"I have to fly today, Linney Bug, because I have a very special passenger. It's a doggie."

Linney wiped her eyes. "A puppy?"

"Well, no, she's fully grown but she was lost and someone here found her and I'm going to fly her back home to be with her owners."

Linney's eyes were suddenly wide with interest. "To her mommy and daddy?"

He hugged her. "Yes, so you see, I have to take her home, but I promise I'll call you when I get there and I'll be home before you know it."

Sophie joined them and offered her a cookie. Linney took it, taking a bite between the hiccups that had started.

"Come on. Let's go get dressed." Katie took her sister's hand and led her upstairs, reminding her of the fun they would have at the clothes closet today.

Zach rested his elbows on his knees. "Maybe I should tell Hank to find someone else," he said to Sophie.

She sat on the coffee table facing him. "No. You need to go. Linney has to learn that people can go away and come home again. It'll take time, that's all. I'll talk to her today and see if I can reassure her."

"Good, because I never know what to say. Talking has never been my thing."

Sophie grinned. "I've noticed. Was that true, what you told her about the dog?"

"Yes, of course. I wouldn't lie to her. Hank helps out an organization called Pilots and Paws. They volunteer their time to fly animals around the country."

Sophie raised her eyebrows. "For vacation?"

He laughed. "No. Mostly it's returning lost pets or pets that have been adopted online and need to be transported to their new owners. Sometimes it's an injured dog that needs to go to a specialized veterinary facility."

A warm light appeared in Sophie's eyes, turning the hazel to a soft shade of green. "That's so very sweet. Have you done this before?"

He shook his head. "It's my first. I never had the time to help out before. It'll be a new experience having a passenger who barks."

"At least you won't have to talk to it." She winked at him as she walked away, leaving him feeling giddy.

But Linney's reaction to his flight lingered in his mind the rest of the morning, intruding into his pre-flight check. It was all he could do to focus and complete the safety check.

Thankfully his furry passenger arrived on time and he was able to lose himself in flying the Citation. Being in the air, above the clouds, defying gravity freed his mind from all problems. He always felt a need to pray, to express his gratitude for the blessings the Lord had given him. Having the chance to raise his brother's kids was an honor and he wanted to do the best job possible. He had a lot to learn, but he knew the Lord would be there to help guide him.

Surprisingly, Sophie had become his guidepost, as well. She pointed out things he could do to deal with unexpected situations. Like calling Linney when he arrived in New Orleans; he wouldn't have thought to do that. She really was amazing with the kids.

She was amazing in a lot of ways.

Sophie's cell rang early the next morning before she'd even dressed. The name on the screen made her smile. Angela. They hadn't spoken in a while and Sophie quickly accepted the call, eager to hear her friend's voice.

"Hi there," Sophie greeted. "How's it going?"

"So…I need to tell you something."

The odd note in her friend's voice triggered some anxiety. "Is anything wrong?"

Angela chuckled. "I hope not. I wanted to be the one to tell you myself. I've put an offer in for your aunt's shop."

Sophie inhaled sharply. "Really? That's great news. You'll make a wonderful owner. Aunt Billie would be so pleased."

"You're not upset?"

"Of course not. I'm thrilled that the shop will be in such good hands."

Angela sighed in relief. "I know you're planning on staying in Mississippi, and I just decided that it was time

I stepped out and took a chance. I've always wanted a business of my own and I love this place."

"I know and I'm so glad you're going to take it over."

"How are things going down there? The store coming along? How's that handsome uncle you told me about? Have you found a place to live yet?"

Sophie pressed her lips together as she sat in the chair by the window. "Things are progressing at the closet. We should start getting the clothes in soon. But I won't be moving down here."

"What? Why not? I thought that was the whole point of the trip. What's happened?"

"Nothing. It's just… I've realized Zach is the perfect person to raise the children. They work well together. They don't need anyone else trying to fit in."

"Sophie, that can't be true. You fit in with everyone everywhere. What's really going on?"

Where to start? "Zach doesn't want me here."

"What makes you say that?"

"He keeps reminding me that my time here is almost over. He keeps saying I must be anxious to get back to where I came from."

"That doesn't mesh with the other things you've told me about him. Are you sure you're hearing him right?"

"That's what he said. What else could he mean?"

Angela chuckled. "Well, he's a man and they aren't the most perceptive people at times. Maybe he's just trying to protect himself. He might be wanting you to stay, but doesn't know how to say that without making it sound like he's pressuring you. He's probably trying to present a confident picture. You know, pounding his chest and proclaiming, 'I'm a man. I can handle three kids without any help.'"

That made sense. Zach was all about being strong and in control. "I suppose that's possible."

"Give it time. Go back to that bridge and ask the Lord for some wisdom and insight. He won't let you down. God brought you there for a reason. You have to see it through to the end."

The conversation moved on, and Angela told her the real estate agent would be in touch with details. When the call ended, Sophie stared at the screen. Her last tie to home was being severed. She was genuinely pleased that her friend would be the new owner of Billie's Boutique Gifts, but it also meant she had no reason to go home.

In the back of her mind she'd always hoped to remain in Blessing. She'd believed that things would work out and she could move here permanently.

But right now that option seemed unlikely.

Sophie strolled into the dressing room area the next day where DJ was busy touching up the girls' paint job. They'd actually done a decent job, though Linney had grown bored long before the job was done.

"Thanks for doing this, DJ."

He shrugged. "No sweat. It's not bad for a couple of squirts."

Sophie grinned. "I agree." She made her way back to the office, checking the art deco clock on the way. The garment fixtures were supposed to be delivered today and she hoped Zach would be here to help.

He'd kept his promise and called Linney yesterday

from New Orleans. She'd been visibly reassured but had been tense until he returned home safely. He'd further distracted her by telling her all about the dog he'd returned to its home and how happy it was to see its owners again.

The girls were with Rachel today so Sophie could focus on the new fixtures and where to place them, which meant they could start bringing in the clothes. The end was in sight. They'd scheduled the grand opening for next week. Rachel had offered to organize the event. Sophie tried not to think about what that day would mean. With the project complete and her gift shop sold as well as her aunt's house, what was next for her?

She glanced out the window at the pounding rain. The storm had come out of nowhere. She was getting used to these pop-up Mississippi thunderstorms. She tried not to think about the last time she'd been here when a storm had blown in and that moment with Zach.

As if materializing from her thoughts, Zach entered the building through the back door. She couldn't stop the smile that took over her face. It happened every time she saw him. She struggled to find something to say. "Thank you again for calling Linney from New Orleans yesterday. It made her feel much better."

He nodded. "I know. She's thanked me, too. But I want to thank you for pointing these things out to me. I want to do right by the kids."

"I know." She shifted uncomfortably. They were smiling at each other like two schoolkids. Thankfully the front door opened and a tall slender man in a baseball cap stepped inside.

"Are you Sophie? Oh my. Of course you are. You look just like your sister."

She'd gotten used to the observation. Everyone in town had known her sister. "That's me."

"I'm Blake Prescott from Retail Supply. My dad asked me to deliver your fixtures since I live here in Blessing."

"Wonderful. I'm glad the storm passed before you got here."

Zach greeted the man warmly. "Blake. Hey, man. Have you given up practicing law to work for your dad?"

Sophie took a second look at the man. "You're an attorney?"

"Guilty as charged. I did a lot of work for Dean's business."

Sophie filed that information away as she instructed Blake where to put the clothing racks. Seeing the silver clothing racks positioned in the main area fueled her excitement. Her sister's dream was coming to life and she had a part in making it happen. Zach and the children had contributed, too, something she knew Maddie would have wanted.

Blake handed her a clipboard to sign for the delivery and she took the opportunity to approach a subject. "I'd like to discuss a legal matter with you. Would you have time to meet with me?"

"Of course." He handed her his business card. "I'll let my secretary know you'll be calling."

Sophie slipped the card into her pocket as Zach approached. "We're entering the final phase. You've done a great job, Sophie. I know Maddie would be proud."

"Thank you. But there's still a lot to do."

"You sound worried. What is it?"

"Someone needs to be in charge of the store and keep it running. It's going to be a lot of work."

"I thought you had volunteers lined up."

"To help, not to take charge." She held his gaze. "I suppose someone will turn up."

"You're probably right. So show me where you want the rest of these racks."

Sophie swallowed her disappointment. She'd hoped Zach would provide the obvious answer to her dilemma but he hadn't even considered it. She shouldn't have been surprised.

Sophie held her phone in her hand later that night, her thumb hovering over Send. Her contest entry was complete. All she had to do was email the picture of her entry to the committee. Today was the final day to enter. She'd worked diligently this past week to complete it. It had proved to be a good way to channel her anxiety over the closet.

A wave of doubt washed over her. There was no real reason to submit this design. She had no chance of winning. But then, she had nothing to lose either. And the mayor had invited her personally to submit an entry.

Taking a deep breath, she hit Send and exhaled slowly. For better or worse it was done now. Maddie wouldn't have had any second thoughts. She'd been fearless and willing to try anything. It was out of Sophie's hands now. She'd wait and see what happened. Her main goal had been to enter the contest. Winning was never her motivation.

Her gaze drifted to her sister's Bible on the side table and the notebook Maddie had written in.

Sophie had found more passages underlined dealing with forgiveness. Maddie's notes tended to focus on that, as well. She'd even listed books about forgiveness she'd wanted to read.

Tears stung Sophie's eyes. If only she was here so she could tell her sister how sorry she was. That she didn't need to find forgiveness in her heart for her little sister. Sophie was to blame.

She stood pacing the room as her emotions bubbled to the surface. If only Maddie had stayed they could have worked it all out. Instead she'd walked out, and found a life of love and happiness with no thought to the people she'd left.

The room closed in around her and she slipped out the French doors and walked across the patio to the yard, stopping at the trellis swing. The evening was balmy and quiet and smelled fresh after the earlier storm. The sounds of night creatures were a welcome alternative to the turmoil in her mind. She sat down and started the swing in motion. The movement began to ease her anger. Why was everything so complicated? She'd come to find her sister and ended up in a mixing bowl of conflict.

She'd found no answers to why Maddie had cut them out of her life, and no idea what her future would be, and her relationship with Zach was a jigsaw puzzle with dozens of missing pieces.

"Sophie. Are you all right? What are you doing out here in the dark?"

She froze. Where had Zach come from? She gritted

her teeth, trying to avoid his gaze, thankful for the darkness. "I'm fine. I had some thinking to do."

He stepped closer, taking hold of the chain that held one end of the swing. She wished he would go inside. His kindness was too much to handle right now. She stood and started to walk away, but his gentle touch on her arm halted her escape and threatened her hold on her emotions.

"Sophie, what is it? Tell me. I can see you're upset about something."

"I'm not upset. I'm angry. No, I'm furious. Why did she leave me behind? Why did she abandon me? I loved her. I needed her." A sob caught in her throat. But she tamped it down. She refused to cry again in front of Zach. He probably already thought she was too emotional.

Zach eased her back onto the swing and sat beside her, resting his arm across the back in a comforting manner and waited.

His silence gave her encouragement. "She must have hated me."

"I doubt that. Maddie didn't hate anyone. Least of all you."

She shook her head. "No. It was my fault. All of it. I'm the reason she left and never came back."

"What do you mean?"

Sophie closed her eyes, reliving that last night. She'd never told anyone about what happened and she didn't want to tell Zach, but his silent support opened the door. Maybe it was time to get this out in the open.

"My mom had gotten really drunk the night before. More than I'd ever seen her. So I poured out all her booze, thinking if she couldn't drink it, she wouldn't be so awful. When she came home, she was furious there was nothing to drink. She blamed Maddie. Mom had never abused us physically, maybe a shove here and there, but she never hit us. She used words and anger as her weapons. That night she attacked Maddie. It was awful. I hid in my room. Maddie came in later and asked me if I emptied the bottles. I admitted it and she left without saying a word. The next morning she left the house and never came back. She took the blame for what I did."

"That's what sisters do. I can think of a few times Dean took the fall for something I did."

Sophie glanced at him. "She hated me for it. All the notations in her Bible and her notebook are about learning how to forgive. She could never bring herself to forgive me for what I did. That's why she left and never contacted me."

"Or...maybe she was struggling to forgive herself for cutting ties. She might have been searching because she was hoping you would forgive her. She's the one who turned away, who denied her family. That must have weighed heavily on her. She must have worried that you might never forgive her, let alone understand."

It was a point of view Sophie had never considered. It fit with what Rachel had shared about Maddie having regrets and failing to deal with old mistakes.

Zach took her hand in his. "Don't be so hard on yourself. You were a kid. Maddie had her own issues. They may have had nothing to do with you. We'll never know. But I know Maddie wasn't a vindictive person."

She stared at their clasped hands. His long fingers

wrapped around her hand infused her with a sense of comfort and security. She didn't want to let go. She met his gaze and her pulse raced. "Do you really think so? I didn't want her to get in trouble. I just wanted Mom to stop drinking."

Zach laid his hand along her cheek. "You did what you hoped would help the situation." His gaze lowered to her lips.

Her heart stopped beating. He was going to kiss her and she wanted him to. But she was also worried that it would change things. If he kissed her, he would claim her heart and she would never get it back. The air crackled between them. Heart pounding, she anticipated his touch. She sensed his shift in mood before he actually backed away and the disappointment washing over her was intense.

She muttered an excuse and hurried across the lawn to the safety of her room. Zach's nearness, the intense attraction pulling them toward each other, flooded her mind. Quickly she prepared for bed, then turned out the light and slid under the covers.

But she knew this complication would rob her of sleep and overtake her dreams.

Chapter Nine

Zach watched Sophie disappear into the house, then sat down on the swing. What had he been thinking? He'd almost kissed her. He'd wanted to. But it would have crossed a line he wasn't ready to cross, let alone acknowledge it existed. She was the children's aunt. Maddie's sister. A kiss would have muddied the waters between them, which would be unfair to the kids. Right now everything was simple and clear, and he wanted it to stay that way.

He started back to the house, glancing at her window as the light suddenly went out. She was probably calling him all kinds of names in her head for his lapse in judgment. Sophie wasn't the kind of woman to be treated casually. Her emotions ran deep and true, and if and when she gave her heart, it would be forever.

That was the scariest part of their whole relationship. The forever factor. She would forever be connected to his family and to him. Nothing would change that. He didn't do forever except with the kids. They were now his forever.

So why did he keep seeing the surprise aunt as a part of his forever future? He knew who he was and he knew he wasn't husband material. That had been pointed out to him often enough. He needed to be content with being a guardian to his kids.

But that didn't mean he couldn't help a friend. Maybe there was something he could do to ease Sophie's concern about the community clothes closet. He'd love to lift some of the burden from her shoulders. She'd been amazing getting the closet completed. He hadn't expected her to be so committed. She'd been a bulldog, never letting any setbacks deter her, always cheerful, positive and making sure the kids were included as much as possible.

That would be his focus now, trying to ease Sophie's concern. Not the swirl of regret that churned in his chest, wishing he'd claimed her kiss.

Sunday arrived, hot and humid, a typical Mississippi morning. Zach parked the car down the block from Blessing Community Church and walked behind the kids as they hurried on ahead. Sophie had gone to the church early to prepare a sign-up table for volunteers willing to help sort and tag the clothes that had been donated to the closet.

His gaze traveled upward to the tall white steeple rising majestically from the roof like a beacon leading the faithful home. It was a treasured landmark of Blessing. Attending services here started his week off with worship and gratitude and gave him the courage to face the week to come.

His brother had urged him for years to reconnect

with his faith. Their father had been a devout man, living his faith daily, and Dean had also been a man of deep faith. Zach had wandered away, embracing the idea that he was in charge of his own life and knew what was best for himself.

It wasn't until his brother had died that Zach realized he had to have more to cling to than his own determination and strength. He needed hope. He needed someone else to be strong. He'd been thrown into the fire, a single guy left with three young kids to raise without a clue how to do that. There was nowhere else to turn but to his heavenly Father.

It had been a humbling and frightening thing, turning his life over to an invisible God, but each day he'd discovered a new purpose, a new reason to embrace his new role and abilities he never knew he had.

Zach entered the foyer of the church and saw Sophie and Rachel seated at a small table signing up volunteers for the closet. She smiled and joked with people who stopped by, her eyes bright with happiness, her smile lighting up the room. It was a far cry from that first day when he'd had to rescue her from inquisitive members.

She caught his eye and waved. He mouthed that he would save her a seat and she nodded in understanding.

He was still reliving that moment last night when he'd almost kissed Sophie. Not exactly the kind of thoughts he should be having in church.

But he had found someone to help lift some of the burden from her pretty shoulders. The woman he'd found was enthusiastic, hardworking and more than qualified to run the closet. He knew Sophie would be pleased with his choice. He smiled, anticipating delivering his news. He looked forward to seeing the relief on her face when she learned what he'd done.

Unfortunately, a last-minute charter flight took him away for the rest of the day, leaving him no time to share his good deed with Sophie. He woke Monday confident that he'd find the right moment. The clothes would start arriving today so Sophie would be at the charity closet all day. He and DJ would be putting the final touches on the checkout counter and securing all the hardware to the doors and cabinetry. There would be plenty of opportunities to talk to Sophie then.

According to the ladies, the sorting and hanging phase would take several days to complete. Zach was grateful he didn't have to get involved with that part of the project. Construction he could handle. Displaying clothing was out of his wheelhouse.

His cell phone rang midafternoon as he was putting away his tools. Zane County Hospital appeared on the screen. Hope soared. As he read the text, a sense of relief washed through him. He took a moment to give DJ instructions, knowing his nephew had learned enough to handle the remaining tasks on his own. He found Sophie and the girls in the corner of the building where a small play area had been set up.

"Sophie. I have to leave for a while. I have an interview with the hospital about the pilot job with their air medivac team."

Her smiled seemed to dim. It was no secret that if she had her way, he'd give up flying completely. That would never happen.

"I see. I hope it works out for you."

"I know you worry about my flying, but this job offers me and the kids security." He took a step toward her. "My job as a pilot is much safer than being a fireman or police officer. You can check the statistics. Pilots aren't hotheaded daredevils who risk their lives doing stupid stunts. Pilots have to be levelheaded, calm, steady and cool in a crisis."

Sophie chewed her lower lip. "I know you'd never do anything to put yourself in jeopardy but the sky is so big and…"

"The plane is so small?"

She grinned and nodded. "It's scary."

"Don't worry. I love the kids. I intend to be more conscientious than ever. Promise." That got him an amused eye roll. He walked off, turning back when she called his name softly.

"Zach, I hope it works out for you."

He smiled. "Thanks. I'll let you know."

Sophie hung four more blouses on the rack, spacing the hangers equally for easy access. It was all coming together thanks to the volunteers who had worked so hard over the last few days. Not to mention Zach and his steady leadership. Her cell phone chimed and she pulled it from her pocket. She didn't recognize the number. She answered it, and when she hung up, her heart was racing and she couldn't help smiling.

Zach noticed and came toward her. "Good news?"

She nodded, unable to stop smiling. "I won the poster contest. They said it captured the essence of Blessing."

A big grin spread across his face. "Congratulations. I'm not surprised, though."

Before she could move, he'd wrapped his arms

around her in a warm hug, stealing her breath. She closed her eyes, enjoying the embrace and wishing it would go on forever. Then he released her, an odd expression on his face. A strained tension pulsated between them, like a plucked violin string. She wanted to believe what she saw in his brown eyes, but deep down she knew he wanted her to leave.

Zach cleared his throat. "This is great news. Your poster will be displayed all over the state. We should celebrate. How about dinner out tonight?"

"Oh, no. They want to present me with the award at the town council meeting this evening."

"Then we'll all be there to applaud. You need your family around you."

Did he really think of her as family? Sometimes she felt as if she'd finally found her place in the world, then he would quickly remind her that her position was temporary. She didn't want to be a temporary aunt. She wanted to be a full-time part of the family. But how much longer would they be her family?

"You should tell the kids, they'll be very proud. I'm proud of you."

She had to smile. "Thank you. I can't believe they picked my drawing." She met his gaze. "I meant to ask you how the interview went. Did you get the job?"

Zach ran a hand along his jaw. "Yes and no."

"What does that mean?"

"They offered me the job but I turned it down."

"What! Why? I thought you said this was the perfect position."

He shrugged. "It turned out to be a back-of-the-clock

shift." He noticed her confusion. "The night shift. That won't work, I need a job with regular daytime hours."

Her heart skipped a beat. She felt his disappointment, but she was also impressed that he'd turned down a job he clearly wanted and would keep him in the air out of consideration for the children. He really was a good guy.

She echoed that thought as she stood smiling at the town council members that evening after receiving her award. Her poster was displayed prominently on the dais and she'd been overcome with a swirling mix of elation and humility. The only thing that kept her standing upright was the sight of Zach and the children smiling at her as if she'd just been crowned queen.

She shook the mayor's hand, then headed toward her family, grateful that the ceremony was concluded. Being in the spotlight was not something she enjoyed.

Linney and Katie hurried toward her with big smiles and hugs. DJ grinned and Zach beamed with pride. For the moment she allowed herself to believe that he cared more than just as a friend and relative.

"I think we need to celebrate. How about ice cream cones and a walk along the river park?"

Zach's suggestion was met with shouts of joy and announcements of what flavors each child planned to order.

A short while later, Sophie savored her black walnut ice cream as they strolled along the riverbank. It was a perfect evening for a walk; a soft breeze stirred the air, laced with the sweet scent of magnolia blossoms. The lights along the walkway reflected in the water. Twinkle lights entwined in the trees added a romantic glow.

With a little imagination Sophie could pretend she was all alone with Zach.

The girls had wandered on ahead to the water's edge and were feeding the ducks. DJ was skipping rocks across the water.

Zach finished his cone and motioned to the bench nestled in between large blue hydrangea bushes near the small waterfall. He took her hand and smiled into her eyes. "I want to tell you again how proud I am—uh, we all are about your winning the contest."

"I'm still surprised. But so honored. I really feel like I'm part of Blessing now." Her drawing had given her a deep connection to the town. At least she'd been accepted by the people of the community.

Zach squeezed her hand. "Of course you're part of Blessing. Everyone admires you for what you've done. I think they talk about you more than they did Madeline. You're practically a local celebrity over this closet ministry."

Her cheeks warmed. "I don't know about that. All I did was finish what my sister started."

"Which is in itself amazing. There are a lot of amazing things about you."

His fingers slowly stroked the back of her hand, making it hard to think clearly and even harder to speak. "I doubt that. I'm just ordinary."

Zach shifted to face her. "You should take a closer look. The woman I see is strong, caring, brave, compassionate and loving."

Was that what he really thought of her? If only it were true, then she'd have hope that her growing feelings for this man weren't in vain. She wished she had the courage to ask him outright, to tell him she was falling in love with him, but she wasn't strong enough to face his rejection.

She braved a look in his eyes and saw that soft light again. He leaned forward. She closed her eyes, only to open them again in confusion when his lips gently brushed her cheek.

His eyes mirrored the confusion jarring her senses. She shifted away, slipping her hand from his. "We should probably go."

He rubbed his forehead. "Um, first I have a surprise for you. I found someone to manage the shop after you're gone."

"What?"

"Nancy Davis. She's a single mom, and hasn't quite accepted yet but I'm sure she will. So now you can breathe easy and not worry about that."

If he'd physically slapped her in the face, he couldn't have hurt her more. "You hired someone without talking to me first? How could you?"

"You were so worried about the future of the clothes closet so I thought I'd take that off your shoulders. I was just trying to help."

Sophie shook her head. "I know what you were trying to do and it had nothing to do with helping. You've made your position clear many times over."

"What?"

"We need to go home. Now." She stood and walked away, fighting to hold back the tears and the pain. She had to face the truth. She was not welcome here. She'd have to make the most of the time left and wipe all thoughts of Zach Conrad from her mind.

* * *

Zach shoved the chocks under the plane's wheels, then locked the door. One of his students had soloed today. That usually made him feel proud. He enjoyed teaching others to fly and knew the deep satisfaction he felt each time he soared in the clouds.

But today instead of heading to his car, he started across the tarmac toward Hank's office in the small blue building that housed the Southland Charters office. He desperately needed advice, and since his friend had been married for nearly twenty years, he had a better grasp on how women worked.

Sophie's flare of anger when he'd shared his news had blindsided him. He didn't understand why she was so upset. He'd expected a big smile, a sigh of relief or maybe even a quick hug.

Hank was on the phone when Zach entered his office. He held up one finger, signaling for him to hold on. Zach helped himself to a seat and waited.

Hank grinned and shook his head. "I don't have any charters for you right now, pal. Sorry."

"I'm not looking for one. I'm looking for some advice."

Hank leaned back in his chair. "Okay. About what?"

"Women."

His friend's loud laughter filled the room. "Then you don't want me. I have no explanation for the fairer sex."

"But you've been married for decades."

"And I don't know much more now than I did on my wedding day. Does this have something to do with the lovely Sophie?"

Zach sighed and shook his head. "I thought I was

doing something nice for her, taking some of the worry over the clothes closet off her shoulders, but when I told her, she was furious. I don't get it."

"What exactly did you do?"

Zach explained, and Hank groaned, tossing him a look of disbelief. "Let me get this straight. You took it upon yourself to hire someone to take over the store Sophie has devoted all her time and energy to and you didn't even get her input?"

"No. I thought it would be a nice surprise."

"Haven't you learned by now? Women don't like surprises. Unless it's flowers or jewelry. Messing with their projects or plans will get you sent to the doghouse." He sighed heavily. "What did she say?"

Zach struggled to recall. "She said she knew what I was trying to do and that I'd made my position clear. Whatever that means. I don't get it. She'll be leaving soon so why does she care who takes over?"

"Are you sure she's leaving?"

"Yeah. She said she'd taken a few weeks off to come down here so she'll be heading home as soon as the store is done."

"That's not what I'm hearing. Paula and Sophie have been spending time together at the store and my wife tells me Sophie would love to stay in town, but she's not sure she'd be welcome."

"Where did she get that idea?"

"Oh, maybe because of something *you* said." Hank stared at him pointedly.

"What? No. I've tried to make her feel welcome. The kids like having her here."

"What about you?"

"She's good with the kids. Better than I am. She fits in well with the family." Too well sometimes. She had a better relationship than he did with the kids.

"Have you told her that?"

Zach shrugged. "Yes. But I don't want to pressure her. I make sure she knows that we'll be okay when she goes home."

"Uh-oh. Have you been telling her it's okay to leave?"

"Not in those exact words, but I guess I've mentioned her leaving a few times."

"Have you mentioned you'd like her to stay?"

"No. That's not my decision."

Hank rested his elbows on the desktop. "Her decision, but you're taking steps to make sure she has no place here by hiring someone else to run the ministry she built, and you don't understand why she was upset? Did it ever occur to you that she might be waiting for some signal from you that she'd be welcome here?"

Zach mulled that over. It didn't make sense. "If she wants to stay, why doesn't she just say so?"

Hank lowered his head and shook it in frustration. "Do you *want* her to stay? Or do you want her gone so you can be in charge of the kids and not have to share them?"

Zach wasn't sure how to answer that. Part of him wanted her to stay. A big part. On the other hand, he couldn't deny his life would be easier if she weren't here. But it would also be missing a big piece of the family.

"I thought so," Hank said at last.

His comment pulled Zach from his thoughts. "What?"

"The fact that you had to think about your answer confirms my suspicions. This is all about your fear of commitment."

Zach stood. "That's ridiculous. I'm fully committed to my kids."

"But not to a woman. That terrifies you, doesn't it?"

He brushed off the observation. "You don't know what you're talking about."

"Prove it. Go tell Sophie that you'd like her to stay here in Blessing. Tell her you have feelings for her—because it's obvious to anyone with eyes that you do—and see what she says."

Zach pointed a finger at his friend. "You are no help at all."

He walked out of the office. Talking to Hank had been a waste of time. He didn't understand his situation at all.

Sophie smiled as another clothes closet volunteer waved hello as she entered the store the next day. She welcomed the distraction of the hustle and bustle of the store. She'd spent the night battling her emotions. Her anger still churned over Zach's ill-advised solution to helping her, and her deep hurt facing the fact that he really did want her out of their lives. Why else would he hire a stranger to manage the store?

The closet looked amazing. Not only was the main floor filled with clothing, but the storeroom in the back was filling up, as well. She couldn't believe how generous the people of Blessing were. They'd gone above and beyond. And it was all because of Madeline's original idea.

There was still one crucial decision to make and Sophie needed the children's input. They needed to choose a name for the store. She'd called the children together and given them each a pencil and paper and instructed them to make of list of possible names. They'd discarded most of them before narrowing it down to three. Maddie's Closet. Blessing Community Closet. Hope Closet. The children would take a vote tonight and make the final decision.

Moving to the front of the building, Sophie smiled at the sight of one of her watercolor posters in the window. She still found it surprising that her simple design had been chosen to represent the upcoming town bicentennial. Seeing her poster displayed in her sister's store made it truly a joint effort. Her sister's dream was becoming a reality.

If only she could be here to see the good it would do and the people it would bless. But Sophie wouldn't be around to see the results. She'd had her heart set on being part of the future of the closet, but she couldn't stay where she wasn't wanted.

Buck came across the room and waved at her, a huge smile on his face.

Sophie grinned. He'd become a good friend through the remodeling process. "You look happy. Did you finally ask Felicia to marry you?" Buck had sought Sophie's advice on his romantic dilemma. He'd been dragging his feet on proposing to his girlfriend for fear she'd turn him down.

"Nope, but I'm working on it. There's a delivery for you. You'll have to come outside to see it."

"What is it? I don't remember ordering anything."

Buck's eyes twinkled. "You didn't. But you're going to like it. A lot."

Sophie followed the carpenter to the back of the building where the exit to the bus platform stood. A large panel van was parked with its back doors wide open. Buck climbed into the van and held out his hand. "You're not going to believe this."

She stepped up into the van and stopped cold. Her hand covered her mouth. "Oh my." A large vintage bus sign with the canine logo leaned against one side. On the other was a set of art deco doors, their angled handles slicing up through the middle of the semicircle glass windows. The epitome of 1920s design.

Sophie ran her hand along the handles. "Where did you find these? They'll be perfect on the front of the store."

Buck chuckled, slipping his hands into his pockets. "These are the original doors. Amos Fisher called me. His dad took the sign when the bus station closed. The doors were removed during a restoration, and he purchased them cheap hoping to find a use for them."

"How much will these cost us?"

"Only a heavy dose of elbow grease. He wanted the outside of the building to look like it did back in the day. He said it would be a gift for the bicentennial."

She smiled up at the carpenter. "I'm thrilled and the mayor will be pleased. Do we have time to put them in?"

Buck nodded. "It might make a little bit of a mess but not too much."

"And what about the old sign? Will you be able to put it back in place?"

"Don't know that yet. I'll have to see if any of the

old support system is still there on the roof, but I'm hopeful."

The surprise gifts chased much of her sour mood away, reminding her that this was about Maddie and the people in Blessing who needed this ministry. That was most important. Not her hurt feelings or fanciful dreams.

Chapter Ten

Sophie winced as she saw Mona Blair, Hank's mother, enter the charity closet the next day. Then worked quickly to adjust her attitude. The woman meant well, bless her heart. She smiled and said hello.

Mona's gaze scanned the area. "I would have thought you'd be further along by now."

Sophie let the dig slide. "Actually, we're right on schedule. It takes a lot of time to get the clothing sorted and hung."

"Hmm." She looked over the rim of her glasses. "Well, I'm sure you know best. I brought y'all some cupcakes from the shop. I figured you'd need a pick-me-up. German chocolate. Hank's favorites."

Cupcakes from Blair's Bakery were a favorite in Blessing. Sophie often wondered how a woman with such a sour attitude could create such sweet and satisfying pastries.

"Thank you. That was very thoughtful."

Mona nodded and scanned the area again. "I wanted to let everyone know how the remodel was coming along. Are you sure you'll be done in time for the grand opening next week? You should have given yourself more time. No need to hurry through this. I'm sure Madeline would have wanted you to take your time."

Sophie smiled between gritted teeth. "I've followed my sister's plan to the letter. Everything is just as she wanted it."

"I doubt that since she's not here to take charge, but I'm sure you did your best."

"I've had a lot of help. The children have especially enjoyed pitching in. It was their idea after all. They really wanted to make their mom's dream come true."

Mona scowled. "I'm not sure I'd call this a dream. We already have stores that collect and distribute clothes for the needy. This seems unnecessary."

Sophie shoved her hands into her pockets. "Those places serve a valuable purpose, but sometimes people need more to get their lives back on track. That's where we come in. We can offer the kind of clothes they need for job interviews."

"Well, I don't see the difference, but I'm not one to criticize. I hear Zach has been deeply involved in this venture, as well."

"Yes. He and DJ have done much of the woodworking in here. DJ has shown a real aptitude for carpentry. His father would be very proud."

Mona huffed. "Well, if Zach had followed through with his agreement, the boy's dad might still be here."

Sophie's heart stopped. "What do you mean?"

Mona stiffened her neck and looked down her nose. "He was supposed to fly Dean and Madeline home from their vacation, but he found something more exciting to do and left them to drive home. That boy was always far too obsessed with airplanes. His parents tried their best to steer him in another direction, but he just had to go his own way."

She picked up her purse. "And look where that got him. Spending the rest of his life trying to make amends. Futile, if you ask me. How can you make up for costing those children their parents? Certainly not by remodeling an old bus station. I hope he can forgive himself one day."

Sophie didn't hear the woman's words as she left. All she could think about was that Zach was somehow responsible for her sister's death. Could he have prevented it? What had really happened?

She'd never asked because she'd assumed it was a simple car accident. But now she wondered what had really happened. Had Zach been lying to her all this time? Was his hard work on the remodel nothing more than trying to appease his conscience? For that matter, was his commitment to the children out of love and devotion or was he doing penance for his poor decision?

A rush of heat shot through her veins. It was time to get the full story of how and why her sister and her husband died. Her heart ached, not only for her loss, but for the discovery that Zach wasn't the man she'd assumed him to be.

Zach knew the moment Sophie walked into the break room that she was fired up about something. Her hazel eyes were shaded toward brown and her lips were pressed into a hard line. Mentally he prepared himself to fix whatever had gone wrong. Was it a problem at the store? Financial problems? Perhaps a lack of volunteers. Whatever it was, he would do his best to make it right. He didn't like seeing her upset. "Hey. Everything okay?"

Her eyes shot bolts of anger in his direction. "We need to talk."

His blood chilled. He could fly a chopper through a fierce Gulf storm, land a fixed-wing aircraft in a blizzard, but facing a woman who wanted to talk scared him. Sophie's angry glare had his mind flashing back to when he'd gotten into trouble as a kid and had to face his dad. A knot of worry formed in his chest.

"You lied to me. Worse, you broke your promise."

"About what?" His mind raced through the last few weeks, trying to see where he might have slipped up.

"How and why my sister and her husband died."

Not what he'd expected. "No. I told you it was a car accident on their way home from Galveston."

"You didn't mention that *you* were supposed to fly them home, but you found something more exciting to do."

His throat seized up, making it hard to swallow. "Who told you this?"

"Mona Blair."

Zach's stomach plunged to his ankles. He should have anticipated this. Miss Mona liked nothing better than expressing her opinion in an effort to stir up trouble. How could he explain so Sophie would understand? "That's not what happened."

"Then explain it to me."

The condemnation in her voice cut deep. He took her arm and steered her into the privacy of the small office.

The hurt and anger in her eyes sliced his heart to pieces. How could he explain it to her when he couldn't understand it fully himself? He turned away, running a hand through his hair. Might as well start at the beginning.

"Maddie and Dean were anxious to spend some time together away from the kids. It had been a difficult winter business-wise and they were eager to find a little peace to regroup. I wanted to save them some money so I offered to fly them to Galveston and then fly them home again when the trip was over."

"You promised?"

Too late he realized he'd chosen the wrong word. Her glacial tone reminded him of her strong opinion about breaking promises. Had he really promised? Or had he merely agreed? He'd promised. Only he hadn't attached much significance to the word until Sophie had come into his life.

"Yes. I did but—"

"You broke your promise and they died."

Zach's emotions sank. "No, that's not what happened."

Sophie crossed her arms over her chest and glared. "So enlighten me."

He struggled to find the right words. The ones that came to mind were weak or flippant, as if he were making excuses. They made him sound like the victim. He took a deep breath, holding tight to the truth and hoping Sophie would understand. "I flew them to Galveston. They were going to call when they were ready to come home."

"Where were the children?"

How like her to think of them first. "My aunt and uncle were here with them. They lived in Blessing at the time."

"Go on."

She wasn't going to make this easy for him.

"I got a call from a buddy in Dallas who worked as a test pilot for a helicopter manufacturer. He was taking a new model up and he invited me along. It was a totally new approach to rotary flight with a fully—"

Sophie held up her hand. She clearly didn't care about the details. "So you found something more exciting to do and broke your promise."

"No. Well, yes, but that's not how it came about. I didn't just not show up. I called my brother and explained the situation. He agreed it was a rare opportunity and that I should go for it. He said they'd rent a car and drive home. He sounded happy about the change in plans. He said it would give them extra time together and prolong the vacation. So I went to Dallas."

"Leaving them to drive home and die on the way. If you'd kept your promise, they would both still be here."

The pain and anguish in her voice knotted his stomach. "It was an accident."

"That could have been prevented if you'd followed through on your obligation."

"I know that." He hadn't meant to raise his voice, but she was prodding his already guilty conscience. "I should have gone to Galveston. But I didn't."

"And now those children are orphans. All alone because you had something more fun to do."

"They aren't orphans. They have me and I'm not going anywhere."

"Because you feel guilty."

"No. Because I *love* them."

Sophie shook her head. "This makes me wonder what

your real motivation is toward the children. Are you here to ease your conscience, hoping to earn forgiveness or are you here out of devotion?"

"I'm here because they're my family. The only family I have. Do I feel guilty for not following through on the flight home? Yes. There's no amount of atonement that will change that or bring back Maddie and Dean."

Sophie looked away. "I thought I knew you. I thought you were sincere in caring for the children, that you were the best guardian for them. Now I'm not so sure."

Zach's blood iced. "What does that mean?"

She wiped her eyes, then turned away. "I don't know."

She walked out, leaving a black cloud descending over his heart and mind. He linked his fingers behind his neck, struggling to find some steady ground.

"Lord, I could use some help here. I don't know how to fix this."

His worst fears had come true. He knew with a sickening certainty that Sophie would try to gain custody now. She'd use his selfish mistake against him and he had no idea how to fight that. But he would.

No one would take his kids away. No one.

Sophie left the store and drove home, struggling to hold it together. Safe in her room, she gave in to the tears. How could Zach do such a thing? She'd questioned his suitability as guardian from the first, but spending time with him at home and working on the closet, she'd discovered a different side to the man. She'd found him caring, patient and devoted to the children. It was obvious they adored him. But how would they feel if they knew he was partially to blame for their parent's death?

She wiped her eyes, her own conscience flaring up. Yes, he'd broken a promise. Yes, he should have followed through on his commitment, but she couldn't actually blame him for the crash. He wasn't driving the car. He'd explained the situation to his brother and been given the go-ahead with his plan.

What she needed now was a fresh perspective. Her emotions were a whirlpool of confusion. She called Angela's number, reaching for a tissue as she waited for her friend to answer.

"Hi! I was just thinking about you. How are things going? Are you ready for the grand opening?"

Sophie couldn't stop the sniffling. "No. Things are awful and I don't know what to do about it." She filled her friend in on the situation between bouts of tears. "How can I ever trust him again? How can I entrust those children to someone who might run off whenever a thrill ride presents itself?"

"How does Zach feel about what happened?"

The questions jolted her from her funk and forced her to step back a little. She thought about the look in his eyes when he'd admitted he'd messed up. The pain and guilt in his dark eyes couldn't be ignored. "He's feeling guilty, I suppose."

"I should think so. What a horrible burden that must be to carry."

Sophie sighed, facing the fact that she hadn't considered his side of things. Now that her anger and hurt were fading, she had to look at things more realistically. "Yes, but he broke a promise and he kept the truth from me."

"Which hurts you more?"

"Both."

Angela made a murmur of understanding. "That's what happens when someone we love disappoints us."

"What are you talking about? I'm not in love with Zach."

"You can keep telling yourself that or you can face the truth. I've known how you've felt since the first week you were in Blessing. Stop trying to put up barriers. Don't be afraid to love again. Greg was a jerk. But Zach isn't like him. He's one of the good ones, but no one is perfect."

Sophie drew her feet up into the chair. "I know that but I don't think I could be involved with someone who breaks his promises."

Angela sighed loudly. "I think you need to take a serious look at your priorities, Soph. I understand why you feel as you do but it's unrealistic. No one intends to break promises but it happens. The Lord's promise is the only one you can count on."

Later, curled up in bed, Sophie tried to deny what Angela had observed, but it was no use. She'd even tried to avoid thinking about it by reading her sister's Bible. Unfortunately, the passage that was underlined was the one in Corinthians that listed all the things that love was and wasn't.

She could no longer deny her feelings. She'd been drawn to Zach from the minute he'd opened the door that first day, despite his dark scowl. There was no denying he was attractive. Dangerously so. She'd tried to ignore the way her heart would flutter when he was near or the silly smile that wanted to erupt whenever she saw him.

They'd developed a comfortable relationship over the time she'd been here. Working at the store, sharing evening meals and spending time with the children. Their time together, the special family moments, inside jokes and amusing comments had bonded them, and she knew a sense of belonging she hadn't known since she and Maddie were young.

So where did that leave her? Stuck between anger and caring. Angela had pointed out that Zach was a good guy. While he might feel guilty, he wasn't responsible for the accident. Dean had been driving the car.

But Angela was wrong about one thing. Breaking a promise was something Sophie could not forgive. Ever. It was a standard she had to hold to. To excuse it now because she was attracted to Zach would go against her deepest convictions.

Besides, it didn't change the fact that Zach had kept the truth from her. What else was he hiding? How was she supposed to have confidence in his role as guardian when he wasn't totally honest? She might be able to pull back on her assessment of Zach as a parent to their nieces and nephew, but how did she retract her feelings for him? How did she wipe that away and how could she care for someone who broke his promises?

Angela was right about one thing. Sophie's heart had opened for Zach and she feared there was no way she could close that door again.

Zach slouched in the patio chair on Hank's large deck the next evening, staring at the lake beyond. The scenic view of the water usually lulled him into a peaceful state quickly. Not today. Even the stunning multicolored sunset splashed across the sky held no wonder for him. His thoughts were consumed with Sophie and her harsh words.

"Here."

Hank handed him a tall glass of sweet tea. His wife, Paula, made the best in town but Zach barely tasted it now. He held the glass, staring into the contents.

Hank took a seat in the chair beside him and waited. It was one of the things Zach liked about Hank. He never pushed. But he wouldn't remain silent forever. Zach rubbed his forehead. He dreaded talking about the accident. He avoided thinking about it as much as possible. But he couldn't do that any longer. Sophie had called him out.

"Sophie found out about me not flying Dean and Maddie home from Galveston."

Hank leaned farther back in his chair. "I see my mother's fine hand in this."

"I don't know how she found out but she's furious. I'm not sure she'll ever talk to me again, let alone trust me."

"It wasn't your fault."

"Maybe not literally, but if I'd followed through maybe—"

"It could have ended the same way. The fault lay with the weather and the truck driver. You've got to stop carrying this guilt around, pal. No one is blaming you for the accident."

"What do I do about Sophie?"

"What do you *want* to do?"

"What do you mean?"

"Does it matter what she thinks?"

"Of course it matters."

"Why?"

Zach had no ready answer. Why did he care? What did it matter? She would be leaving soon. End of problem. He squirmed in his seat. When had he started lying to himself? "Because she's the kids' aunt. She's family."

"Is that the only reason?"

"Of course. What else could it be?"

"How do you really feel about the lovely Sophie?"

Zach stood up and walked to the edge of the deck. Why did Hank always call her *the lovely Sophie*? "I don't have any feelings. I mean, I like her, we're friends. We both want the best for the kids."

"You are more dense than I ever believed. You care about her. A lot. Why can't you admit that?"

Zach knew his friend was right but he wasn't ready to go down that road. Admitting his growing feelings for the surprise aunt would force him to face that she was a better guardian. That she knew the kids better than he did, that he was a failure. He'd tried for months to be the man they needed. Sophie had breezed in and made them all a family with her smile and her caring heart and her understanding of what the kids were going through.

He was in no way equipped to maintain the family on his own.

Hank spoke softly, his wise words falling over Zach like a friendly touch.

"You have to forgive yourself. The Lord may forgive us and forget, but He lets us remember so we can be reminded of our mistakes and avoid them in the future and maybe help someone else down the road. You're a great parent, Zach, and you'll be a great husband one day. Don't run away from love because you're afraid you'll fail. You didn't fail Maddie and Dean. You won't fail the kids either."

Zach set his flight bag on the floor and made a bee-line to the coffeepot.

Sophie glanced up from the breakfast table. "Are you flying today?"

Zach joined her, lifting a sugar donut from the plate. His favorite. Sophie was a very observant woman. She'd picked up on his taste for donuts and had started surprising him with them once a week. It was amazing how she had figured him out without any questions or pestering. He liked that.

"Yes. I have to fly to Phoenix but I should be back by early evening. What do you have on tap for today?" He tried to make his tone light and casual, but he and Sophie had hardly spoken since she'd learned of his part in the accident. It had been the longest two days of his life.

Sophie wiped the counter, keeping her back to him. "We're finalizing the plans for the grand opening next week. I'm working on the ad campaign for the *Blessing Bugle*. DJ is going to help me with hanging a few pictures and shelves."

A warm rush entered Zach's chest. "He's turning into a fine young man."

"Yes, he is." She turned to face him. "He looks up to you, you know. Working on the closet has given him a new outlook."

He nodded, holding her gaze. "Thanks to you. You were right all along about the project being good for the kids. I didn't see it but you did."

She looked away.

Linney came over and leaned against his side and he slipped his arm around her. "Are you leaving again?"

"Only for a short time. I'll be home around suppertime."

Linney gave him a pitiful look. "Do you *have* to go?"

He tapped her nose with his finger. "Yes. It's my job, remember? We talked about this."

"I know. You'll be careful, won't you?"

"I pr—" He glanced at Sophie. "Of course I will. I'm always careful." He kissed the little girl's forehead. "Are you going to help your aunt today?"

A big smile replaced her worried frown. "We're planning a big party for the store. Everyone will be there. It's going to be awesome."

He had no doubt. Anything Sophie organized would be amazing.

Katie and DJ drifted into the kitchen as Zach finished his morning coffee. "DJ, would you finish attaching the cabinet pulls in the storeroom? You can use my drill if you'd like."

"Yes, sir. I can handle it."

"I'd better get going. Y'all have a good day at the store. I'll check it out when I get back."

Sophie followed him to the back door. "Thank you for not promising Linney you'd be careful. I know it might seem like a picky point to you, but keeping a promise is a serious thing to a child."

"I remember."

A smile brightened her delicate features and put a sparkle in her eyes. For a moment he allowed himself to think the light was because of him. Because she cared. A little. "Be safe, Zach. We want you back."

"I want to come back. That's the best incentive of all."

Her smile widened, filling him with a buoyancy he'd not known since he was a kid. It lingered on the drive to the airfield and kept his spirits floating when he took off for the return flight late that afternoon. He was anxious to see Sophie and the kids. He couldn't remember a time when he'd been looking forward to going home as much as he did today. Normally he was itching to get away, back in the cockpit and out of the dull domesticity that had always choked him.

Twenty miles out from the county airfield, he encountered bad weather. Maintaining control of his aircraft took his full concentration and a few fervent prayers. He might not have literally promised his family he'd return, but he wasn't about to mess up.

The storm was in full force as he hurried to his car. He could have waited it out, but the need to see Sophie and the kids was too strong.

He was approaching the city limit sign when his tire blew, jerking the car to the right and down into the ditch. The airbag deployed, slamming against him with surprising force. His head erupted in pain, then darkness. His last thought was that he had to get home.

Chapter Eleven

Sophie glanced out the office window of the closet at the steady rain predicted to last through the evening, trying not to think about Zach navigating his plane through the bad weather. He was a grown-up and by his own admission an excellent pilot.

Despite her determination to dismiss Zach from her mind, her concern grew steadily through supper and early evening when he failed to arrive home. He'd been certain he'd be back around mealtime. Fortunately, the children had been so busy they hadn't asked about him. However, she noticed that Linney was starting to get edgy. She was looking toward the door every few minutes.

Sophie sent up a prayer that Zach would arrive soon, and that he was all right. She may be furious at him but she didn't want anything to happen to him either.

When the children settled in to watch a movie later that evening, Sophie sought some quiet time on the front porch swing. The movements soothed her anxious mood. She still had no word from Zach and it was getting late. What if something had happened to him? The thought chilled her to the bone.

When her cell suddenly chimed, her pulse spiked. Zach. She held her breath as she answered. "Where are you? Is everything all right?"

The long pause before he answered stole her breath from her lungs.

"I'm at the hospital. But I'm fine. Just a few bumps and bruises."

She gasped. "What happened? Did you crash?"

"Yes, but not the plane. My car got a flat and ended up in the ditch. Thankfully a Good Samaritan saw the whole thing and called an ambulance. I need you to come get me since I don't have a car."

"I'll be right there. I'll call Rachel to stay with the children." She ended the call and dialed her friend as she went back inside to get her purse. Rachel arrived within minutes. She realized that she had to tell the children something, but she didn't want them panicking.

"Children, I need to talk to you a minute."

They glanced up at her, their expressions puzzled, and Sophie scrambled to come up with an explanation. "Uncle Zach had a flat tire on the way home from the airfield and he needs me to pick him up. We'll be home as soon as possible. You behave for Miss Rachel."

Between traffic lights, slow drivers and an ambulance, the drive to the hospital took longer than normal, further scraping her already raw nerve endings.

Zach was waiting just inside the emergency room door when she arrived, and her first sight of him wrenched her heart. She approached him slowly. Her hand went up to touch the long bandage on the side of his face partially covering his left eye. His right cheek was puffy and his bottom lip was cut.

He shrugged. "Airbag. And a hard hit to my thick skull." He held up a small plastic bag. "My meds, and I have a slight concussion."

Sophie took his arm. "Do you need to stay awake? We have things to talk about."

He gave her a guilty expression. "I suppose we do. I was afraid you wouldn't come when I called you."

The thought never occurred to her. All she could think about was Zach being hurt. "Of course I would. We're family."

"Yeah. We are."

The drive home passed in silence. Sophie kept waiting for Zach to say something, but he spent the time staring out the window. He looked awful and her heart pinched when she thought about what might have happened. "Are you in much pain?"

He chuckled softly. "No. I think they gave me some heavy-duty painkillers. They did warn me to take them regularly because when they wear off, I won't be happy if I miss them."

"I'll make sure you take them on time. Anything else I should know?"

"No. I need to make an appointment with my regular doctor to follow up on the injuries. No big deal."

Sophie measured her next words carefully. "I'm glad you weren't seriously hurt."

Zach glanced in her direction but she kept her eyes on the road ahead. The rain was still coming down steadily. "I know. I have to admit there was a Jesus-take-the-wheel moment when the car was heading into the ditch."

Sophie had called on Jesus a few times on the drive over. "You need to be very reassuring to the children. I don't know what Linney will do when she sees your injuries."

"I've thought about that. I'll make sure I have a big smile on my face."

She looked over at him and his swollen eyes and lip. "Won't that hurt?"

"Probably, but I don't want to upset the kids."

Zach moved stiffly as they made their way up onto the back porch. She could see he was feeling the results of the impact. The kids looked up when they entered the family room. Rachel's mouth opened in surprise.

"Uncle Zach. What happened?" Katie asked.

Linney's eyes teared up. "Why are you hurt? Why is your face all messed up?" She rushed to his side and grabbed his hand, her sweet face distorted with worry.

He picked her up and gave her a kiss. "I'm fine, Linney Bug. My car went into a ditch when I got a flat tire. Just some scratches and bruises from the airbag. I'm fine."

DJ smirked. "You look like a cage fighter."

"I'm sure I do."

Katie hugged him around the waist. "Are you sure you're okay?"

"Absolutely, Katie Belle. But I am tired, so I think I'll sit in my recliner."

"I'll help you." Katie guided him across the room.

Rachel steered Sophie into the kitchen. "Are you sure he's okay? He looks awful."

"He says he is. He has to meet with his regular doctor and he has to stay awake tonight but I think he'll be fine."

"How are you?"

"Me? I'm fine. Why wouldn't I be?"

Rachel lifted her brows. "Uh, because the man you care for was in an accident. That kind of thing can shift your thinking."

"I don't know what you're talking about."

Rachel grimaced. "Still in denial, huh? Okay. I'll leave it for now, but you need to do some soul-searching, my friend, and face the truth."

As she got the children into bed, Sophie couldn't shake Rachel's comments. Angela had also suggested that her feelings for Zach went deeper than she realized. Yes, she cared for him, she might even be falling in love with him, but that didn't mean she loved him the way they were thinking.

Zach had his eyes closed when she returned to the living room. She touched his forearm.

He opened his eyes and looked directly into hers. A warm light softened the dark gaze and a smile moved his lips. "Sophie. What a sweet sight to wake up to."

Her throat tightened. He was on medication. He didn't know what he was saying. She tried to not think about how much she wished he meant what he'd just said.

His gaze sharpened and he nodded. "Maybe we should watch a movie or something."

Sophie took a seat at the end of the sofa nearest his chair so she could keep watch but that proved harder than she'd expected. They watched a movie, caught up on sports news and ate a light meal. He resisted taking his pain meds but she held her ground. Throughout the whole night, Rachel's advice swirled in the forefront of her mind.

She didn't have to look hard to face the truth. She was in love with Zach. Not sure how it happened or when, but taking care of him, watching over him, made her realize she wanted to do it forever. She wanted to face each new day with him at her side and confront each life challenge as a team. Mostly she wanted to raise the children with him. They both loved them completely. And she loved him with all her heart.

She buried her hands in her face a moment, then glanced at Zach who was channel surfing again. What would he say if she told him how she felt? He'd probably be embarrassed and avoid her for the next week.

She knew he was attracted to her. But attraction wasn't love, and she would settle for nothing less. She feared that love and commitment weren't traits that Zach had cultivated.

She'd have to settle for friendship.

Not sure she could do that.

Zach slid behind the wheel of his SUV and shut the door. The silence was welcome, but it failed to shut out the words of the doctor. His follow-up visit to his GP had resulted in him being sent to an ophthalmologist. He hadn't anticipated any real issues but the examination today had left a cold knot in his chest.

There was a serious problem with the retina in his right eye. It was repairable with surgery but there was no guarantee. However the problem was serious enough to urge surgery as soon as possible. If it wasn't taken care of quickly, it could lead to a loss of vision in that eye down the road.

Neither option appealed to Zach but he couldn't ignore the situation. Having an operation on his eye was a terrifying prospect, but losing his vision, never being able to fly again, was worse.

He wished he could talk it over with Sophie but she'd only worry. And there was no way he would tell the kids. Memories of how upset the girls were when he missed Katie's birthday party still troubled him. He would never put them through that again and he wasn't going to risk scaring them with news of his eye surgery.

There was only one logical course of action. He'd keep the surgery a secret until he knew the final outcome.

He started the car and headed out of the large parking garage turning toward the highway to make the two-hour drive back to Blessing. He'd analyzed the various outcomes a dozen times by the time he neared home. The green landmark sign for the Blessing Bridge rose in the distance as if reminding him who he should consult.

Parking in the small lot, he made his way down the pathway. The midday heat was tempered somewhat here beneath the canopy of trees. He stood in the middle of the old weathered bridge, staring into the still water of the lake below. A frog leaped from the underbrush into the water, sending ripples across the sun-dappled surface.

He could find no words to begin his prayer. All his life he'd wanted to fly. It defined him. Losing that ability would be like ripping his heart from his chest. But losing vision in one eye was equally terrifying.

An image of Sophie floated through his thoughts. She'd been against his flying career, concerned that it was too dangerous. He'd resented her opinion. She'd probably be relieved if he could no longer fly. She'd blame his accident for the eye problem, but the doctor had reassured him that nothing had caused this problem. It was just something that happens. So where did that leave him?

Why are you doing this to me, Lord? Why now?

He closed his eyes, hoping for answers, some sign or a whispered word that would give him courage and show him the direction. Since Dean and Madeline's deaths, his life had been like trying to balance a board on a basketball. Always tilting, struggling to remain on an even keel, never feeling secure. He'd tried to regain a measure of control but it always remained out of reach.

Zach opened his eyes. He'd found no answers at the bridge today. No whispered word from above, no scripture came to mind, no sudden spiritual insight. Discouraged, he started back down the path to the car, the tune of the old hymn "Trust and Obey" playing in his mind. He shook his head. Was that his takeaway? If so, it wasn't much comfort because he had never been good at either of those traits.

For the time being, he'd stick to his original plan and keep the medical news to himself. There was nothing to be gained by upsetting everyone. The opening of the store was scheduled for the day after tomorrow. Once that was over, he'd examine the situation and go from there.

Right now the grand opening was paramount. Nothing could go wrong. He'd told Hank not to schedule any flights for him that day. The day was all about Sophie. She deserved all the credit for the closet opening and he looked forward to seeing her hard work rewarded.

The solitude of the master bedroom welcomed Sophie along with the sweet companionship of Lumpy who had followed her. She stroked his silken fur and curled up in the swivel rocker near the window, picking up her sister's Bible. Lumpy snuggled at her feet, offering his brand of quiet comfort.

Once again her emotions were pulled in two directions. Zach was none the worse for wear after his collision in the ditch. But her heart was still sore from learning about Zach keeping silent about his part in her sister's death.

But Sophie had come to Blessing to find answers and uncover the reason her sister had turned her back on her family. She understood that Maddie had found happiness in her marriage and her own family. She accepted her sister had carved out a fulfilling life in this community, but reading through her sister's Bible notations and her entries in her personal notebook, she'd found no explanation. Madeline had mentioned her name several times but with no comments, as if she'd thought of her, then forgotten her in the next moment.

Sophie clung to Rachel's suggestion that Maddie had found it hard to reach out to her younger sister, and as time moved on, it had become more and more difficult. Sophie had been to the Blessing Bridge and prayed for an answer. She'd prayed for insight each Sunday during the service but so far she was still in the dark.

Pulling open the small drawer in the side table, she reached for a pencil. She'd started making her own notations in the Bible as she read, marking passages that spoke to her and gave her comfort.

Her finger snagged a piece of paper she'd not noticed before. She pulled out a small card with a picture of morning glories climbing a rustic post. Her favorite flower. Maddie always teased her about being a morning glory person, always in a good mood when she woke up each day.

Sophie opened the card. All it said was Thinking of You. Her heart shrunk. No message, no salutation. Had the card been for her? She glanced into the drawer again and pulled out the envelope. Her name was written on it, as if Maddie had intended to write the entire address.

Had that been her intention? Had she wanted to reach out? Why hadn't she? What held her back? Didn't she understand that Sophie would have forgiven her anything? Nothing could be worse than the years of not knowing, the burden of guilt she'd carried and the giant hole in her heart that nothing could fill.

Slipping the card into its envelope, she tucked it in the middle of the Bible. For now she'd choose to believe that Maddie had intended the card for her, that she would have sent it with words of love and reconciliation.

Zach walked into the kitchen the next evening as Sophie was opening the pizza box. "Hope you're in the mood for sausage and pepperoni," she said. "We were busy at the store all day."

He grinned trying to act normal. "I'm always in the mood for pizza. How are things going for the grand opening?"

"Good. There's still a lot more to do."

He smiled. Sophie always worried that things wouldn't get done but somehow she never failed to meet her deadlines. "What can I do to help?"

She thought a moment, then shook her head. "Nothing really. The women of the church are helping, but thanks."

Linney lifted a piece of pizza from the box and laid it on her plate. "Do we get to come to the grand opening?"

Sophie chuckled. "Of course. I need you to help hand out the refreshments."

"What's that?"

DJ piled three pieces on his plate. "Snacks, silly."

Katie slid into her seat and reached for a slice of pizza. "What can I do?"

Sophie took a sip of her drink. "You can be one of the hostesses that greet people at the door and hand out the information sheets."

"Cool. What about Uncle Zach? What's he going to do?"

Zach raised his eyebrows. "What do you have in mind for me?"

A faint blush tinged her cheeks. "He can do whatever he wants."

Katie glanced between them as if sensing something was off. "But you'll be there, won't you, Uncle Zach?"

"Of course. I've worked hard on that store. I want to be there to see it open."

"Promise?"

Zach tapped the end of her nose with one finger. "I promise I will be there. Nothing will stop me. I even told Mr. Hank not to schedule any charter flights for me that day just to make sure." He glanced at Sophie, hoping she could hear the sincerity in his voice.

She smiled and he sighed in relief. She trusted him. That was a huge victory. After the disagreement over his part in Dean and Maddie's fatal accident, he feared their old relationship was destroyed.

Zach finished his pizza, watching Sophie move about the kitchen, his conscience stirring. Maybe keeping his medical problem a secret wasn't such a good idea. The last time he'd tried that, it had exploded in his face.

When the kids went to watch TV in the family room, he remained at the breakfast table, waiting for an opportunity to talk to Sophie. He'd feel better if she knew what was going on. Sharing his concerns with her might help his own anxiety, too.

Sophie set the empty pizza box on the counter, then sat down at the table. "Can I talk to you a minute? I need some advice."

Her question caught him by surprise. She had never sought his advice before. She was usually handing it out. "Of course."

She traced a line in the wooden table with her finger as if collecting her thoughts. "I found a card in my sister's drawer. It wasn't signed but it had a picture of my favorite flower on it and inside it said Thinking of You. She'd written my name on the envelope." She met his gaze, her blue eyes clouded with sorrow. "Do you think she might have planned on sending it to me and just never had a chance?"

The need to comfort and reassure her was fierce. He knew how important it was for her to understand why Maddie had walked out without a word. He searched for something encouraging to say. "I think it's possible. I don't know why your sister behaved as she did, but I know she was a good woman, someone who cared deeply for everyone. I'm sure she cared for you very much."

Sophie rubbed her lower lip. "Then why did she stay away?"

Zach reached over and took her hands in his. "Maybe for the same reason I didn't tell you about me not flying Dean and Maddie home. I didn't want to face my part in the whole thing. It was easier to hide it away and not think about it. Maybe Maddie was too ashamed to reach out, and the longer it went, the harder it became."

"Rachel said the same thing."

The break in her voice sliced into him. He wished he could solve this problem for her, give some kind of definitive answer, but there was none. "I'm sorry."

Sophie slipped her hands from his and blinked away tears. "I guess I'll never know why."

"You knew your sister better than anyone, despite all the years apart. What do you think she meant to do with that card?"

"I want to believe she was going to send it to me."

"I do, too. Then let's choose to think that."

The smile she gave him was worth everything he had. "Thank you. You eased my mind."

Zach remained seated after Sophie left the room. He'd intended to tell her about his eye problem but now he wasn't so sure. She had enough weighing on her

mind. Adding to her burden would serve no purpose.
He'd keep his troubles to himself until he knew the outcome. It would save everyone a lot of worry.

All thoughts of his medical problems faded into the
background in the rush to get the grand opening program ready. Sophie had invited local government offi-
cials and the heads of the Blessing service organizations
to attend. The local pastors were to be present as well,
to add their prayers to the event.

Midafternoon, Zach's phone rang. Jackson Vision
Care. He exhaled a slow breath before answering. When
he hung up a few moments later, he wished he had ignored it.

The doctor had scheduled his surgery for the next
day. The day of the grand opening. He'd tried to reschedule it, but the physician was adamant.

Zach scanned the store. Everything was nearly ready.
Sophie darted around, making sure everything was per-
fect. It was her big day. He'd promised her he'd be there.
He'd promised the kids, too.

His mind searched frantically for a way out. Telling
Sophie now about his surgery would ruin the grand
opening for her. He'd never forgive himself if he had a
hand in that. But breaking his promise to Sophie would
mean the end to any hope of a relationship between
them.

Slipping out the back door, he drove to the airfield
and parked at Hank's office. He needed a plan and he
needed an accomplice. And he needed the good Lord
to keep His hand on him good and tight.

Chapter Twelve

Zach fastened his seat belt, trying not to think about the outcome of this surgery. His doctor was optimistic but he'd also laid out all the risks involved. Risks that could mean the end of his career as a pilot.

Hank glanced over at him from the driver's seat. "I'm still not sure this is a good idea. Why not just tell Sophie and the kids that you need surgery?"

"Because there's no need for them to know. You didn't see how upset they were after that night I was late getting home. The girls were terrified that I wouldn't come home again, and before my next charter, Linney begged me not to go. There's no point in getting everyone upset. Once it's all settled, then I'll explain."

Hank started the car and shook his head. "I think you're making a mistake. What if the surgery runs late? You'll miss the grand opening. That won't go over well."

Zach stared out the side window, his thumb worrying his lower lip. "Yeah. I know."

"Couldn't you have rescheduled the operation?"

"I tried but the doctor said it needed to be done immediately. I had no choice." He'd gone over it a dozen times in his mind and waiting to explain to the family was the only sensible approach. Of course if the procedure didn't go well, then he'd have a whole new set of issues to face, but he didn't want to think about that possibility.

He glanced at his watch. The surgery was scheduled for eleven thirty and would take half an hour start to finish. If all went well, he'd be on his way home by noon. Allowing for the two hour drive back to Blessing from Jackson, he should be there in plenty of time to attend the opening. The only thing he'd have to explain would be the patch over his eye. He was holding to the old adage that it was easier to ask forgiveness than seek permission.

But if he didn't return in time, he stood to lose everything. He'd promised the kids and Sophie he'd be there. He'd believed it at the time. Breaking his promise was the ultimate crime to Sophie, and the kids would never trust his word again.

Maybe Hank was right. Maybe he should have told them. The memory of Linney and Katie's hysterics that day were never far from Zach's mind. He could never put them through that again. His heart wouldn't survive.

And Sophie—the condemnation in her hazel eyes would shred his being. There was no way he could explain or make it up to her, she'd never forgive him. He'd lose her forever. It was his fault for allowing himself to fall in love with her. He hadn't meant for it to happen. It had crept up on him steadily, inch by inch, like a kudzu vine, until his whole being was hopelessly entangled.

He'd wanted to speak to her, to tell her how he felt,

but there was never a quiet moment or the appropriate time. Then when he'd found an opportunity, his courage failed him and he let the moment slip from his grasp.

"So what's your cover story? Where are you supposed to be?"

Zach exhaled a sigh. "I left her a note saying I was going with you to check out a helicopter you were thinking of buying for the business."

"What? I would never buy one of those flapping bag of bolts."

"What did you tell your wife?"

Hank scowled. "The truth. That I'm driving you to Jackson for eye surgery. But she has instructions to tell everyone I have business in Biloxi."

"I suppose we should have gotten our stories straight."

"Nah. It'll be fine. If everything goes as scheduled."

That was the thing Zach feared most. Closing his eyes, he offered up a prayer for things to go according to plan. If they did, Sophie would only be upset that he'd kept his surgery a secret.

One good thing. His concern over missing the opening outweighed his own anxiety about the surgery and its outcome. He could be facing a life without flying. The idea knotted his stomach and left a hollow ache inside his chest.

He was a born flyer. The only time he felt whole and free was in the air. No matter what kind of aircraft he was in. Without his ability to fly, he had no identity.

First things first. Surgery, then see what happens after that.

Hank dropped Zach at the surgery center, then went to park the car. After checking in, Zach took a seat and waited. An hour and forty-five minutes past his scheduled surgery time, he was still waiting. Every minute that passed, he recalculated the time needed to be in Blessing for the opening. Sophie had worked so hard on this closet project, the kids, too. He needed to be there, but he needed to take care of his vision first.

Finally, his name was called. But he was well behind schedule and the chances of keeping his promise were fading fast.

His heart began to crack. He'd lost Sophie forever.

Sophie applied a few strokes of blush to her cheeks, then took a quick survey of herself in the mirror. She'd discarded three outfits before deciding on a simple blue dress and small necklace. She wanted to look professional but not fussy. Her stomach fluttered as she thought about the grand opening. In under an hour it would be in full swing. It wasn't the event that made her anxious but the fact that Zach wasn't home yet.

He'd left a note this morning telling her he and Hank had gone to Jackson to see about a helicopter Hank wanted to buy, but he assured her he'd be home in plenty of time for the opening. The note had triggered memories of another time he'd chased after a helicopter instead of attending to his duty. Though he had no duty toward her or the store, he had still promised.

She couldn't think about that now. She had a grand opening to host. The closet was all about her sister's memory. Everything else would have to wait.

Sophie steered her car toward downtown but at the intersection she turned the opposite direction. She needed to make a stop at the bridge.

Her heart was troubled and she needed some clarity and strength for the rest of the day. She wanted to stay with the children. She wanted to stay in Blessing, but at the moment she saw no way that would happen. She knew from experience that the Lord could sort out the most complicated situations and the most dire of crises.

She left the bridge not with hope so much as a tight grip on God's promise to work all things for good. Whatever that might turn out to be. Tomorrow she would have faith and leave it in His hands.

An hour and a half later, Sophie's faith was fading. In half an hour, the opening would be over.

Zach wasn't here. He hadn't called or answered his cell phone. She'd tried to remain calm and hopeful and give him the benefit of the doubt, but the opening would be over soon. Her emotions pitched between burning anger and wrenching disappointment.

She fought her anxiety and smiled as yet another Blessing resident entered the charity closet. She thanked them for their presence and well wishes, then directed them toward the refreshment table where the ladies of the Blessing Community Church had donated an assortment of pastries and sweets. The generosity of this town never ceased to amaze her.

If the attendance at this opening was any indication, Maddie's Closet would benefit many people in Blessing. Her spirits lifted when she thought about all the good the charity would do and how gratifying it would be seeing lives altered with a simple change of clothes... except, she wouldn't be here to see it.

Sophie stepped away into the quiet of the small office. It was time to face a few hard facts. There was no permanent place for her here. Zach had the family in good hands. She didn't have to worry about that any longer. From here on, her place in the family would be relegated to visiting aunt. The woman who dropped in on holidays, then flew off home again.

Sophie wrapped her arms around her waist. What she couldn't push aside was the fact that Zach had failed to show up. How could he do this to the children after he'd promised to be here? She'd believed that he'd finally come to understand the importance of keeping promises. He'd told her that he wouldn't let anything keep him from the opening. He wouldn't have promised if he wasn't sure.

She didn't want to believe she'd misjudged him again, but his absence was proof enough. So much for her judgment of people. Of men. The pain around her heart squeezed tighter. What a fool she was. She'd believed him, trusted him. Tears stung the backs of her eyes but she brushed them quickly away. He wasn't worth it.

Rachel tapped on the door frame. "Are you all right? People are asking for you."

"I'm coming." She forced a smile and faced her friend.

Rachel came closer, resting a comforting hand on her back. "What is it? Zach?"

Sophie nodded. "He promised he'd be here. He *promised*."

"There's still time."

She shook her head. "He's not who I thought he was. I should never have believed him."

"Don't you think that's a bit unfair? I mean, anything

could have happened. I don't want to be gruesome, but there could have been an accident."

"No. Nothing ever happens to Zach. Even after his wreck, he emerged with only a few bumps and bruises." The harsh tone of her voice surprised her but her disappointment was growing.

"How long have you been in love with him?"

"What?" She turned away. "Don't be ridiculous. I'm not in love with Zach."

Rachel chuckled softly. "I think it happened sometime around the point you saw Zach teaching DJ carpentry."

She tried to deny it but couldn't. That had been a turning point of sorts. His kindness and patience with the boy had touched her heart and she'd started to notice other small moments of tenderness he expressed toward the girls. Even Lumpy had been the recipient of some special attention. She'd had to acknowledge that Zach might be inexperienced, but she couldn't question his devotion to the children.

"Even if that were true, I can't forgive him for breaking a promise."

"I think you're asking the impossible. No one intends to break a promise, Sophie, but life happens. Unexpected things crop up. Why is keeping a promise so important?"

"Because everyone in my life broke their promises and I ended up all alone."

Rachel nodded. "I'm sorry you had to go through that. I doubt any of those people intended to let you down. There are a lot of things in our lives that are out of our control. Is it possible that you're using this promise gauge as a way of protecting your heart? It gives you a reason not to love someone, to keep from getting hurt." Rachel gave her a little hug. "No one is perfect, sweetie. We all fail. I'll bet if you think about it, you've broken a few promises yourself. Don't forget, forgiveness is a two-way street."

Sophie set aside her concerns over Zach and rejoined the crowd in the store. The opening was winding down and it was time to wind down her hopes, as well. Zach Conrad couldn't be trusted. He wasn't a forever kind of man. He was a man who avoided commitment. A man who lost focus when something more exciting than the opening of a charity closet came along.

Sophie closed the front door of the shop, dimmed the lights and retreated to her small office. The opening had been a huge success. The offers of donations and help would guarantee the closet's success for the near future. There was nothing more she could do here. Refusing offers to help clean up, she welcomed the solitude the empty store offered. With each scrap of food she tossed, each spill she wiped up, a piece of her heart tore away.

Standing in the vacant store, the significance of her loss settled over her like a heavy blanket. She dropped onto one of the wooden benches, too heartbroken to even cry.

Why had Zach broken his promise? Was a helicopter so important that he missed this event and hurt her and the children? How could she have been so wrong about him?

But was she? She accused him of being unable to commit. But that wasn't true. He had committed totally to the kids. He'd walked away from his dream job because it would have been wrong for the kids. He'd committed to the remodel and followed through to the end.

Had she put too much emphasis on keeping promises? Had any of the promises broken for her been deliberate? Or had they come about from a sudden change in circumstances? Maddie hadn't known that her mother would get so angry and push her to move out. Her father hadn't planned on leaving her with her aunt, but she'd learned later that he'd lost his job and had to move away to find another one. She'd forgotten that.

Greg had promised to love her forever, but if she were honest with herself, she'd always known he didn't mean it.

What about her own promises? Had she broken any? She'd always tried to honor her word but there had been a few times when illness had prevented her from attending a special event for a friend. When Aunt Billie had become ill, she'd had to reschedule several things she'd promised to take care of. How had she forgotten those incidents?

She'd broken a sacred promise but the world hadn't come to an end. Life had gone on. Her friend had understood, and the event had gone on without her and Aunt Billie had deeply appreciated her care.

Was Rachel right? Was Sophie using her high standards to keep from being hurt again?

She placed her elbows on the desk and cradled her head in her hands. Was she really that weak and fearful that she'd create ridiculous barriers to keep people at bay?

She could no longer deny the truth. The memory of her past pain had been like a permanent thorn in her heart. But no one had broken their promises simply to hurt her.

Why had it taken her to age thirty-one to see the truth?

Her gaze lowered to the desktop; the smooth satin finish reminded her that Zach had built it for her, tangible evidence of his commitment to the store. Maybe he had a good reason for not being here. The least she could do was wait and hear his side of the story.

If she'd learned nothing else through the ups and downs of working on her sister's dream, it was that she had to roll with the punches. Rachel was right, forgiveness worked both ways. People make mistakes; you couldn't hold a grudge, and you couldn't expect everyone to be perfect.

Zach stared out the car window, his mind replaying scene after scene of things he'd lost today. Mostly he saw Sophie, angry, turning her back on him, withholding her forgiveness forever.

Withholding her love.

He exhaled. He'd known he was falling for Sophie but he hadn't recognized the moment when he'd handed her his heart. Maybe Hank was right. Telling Sophie up front about his retina problem and surgery might have changed everything.

But the truth would have terrified the kids and left Sophie worried and preoccupied on her important day. The closet meant everything to Sophie. If he'd learned nothing else, he knew Sophie took other peoples' problems to heart. She would have worried about him and about his ability to care for the kids.

"What do you think Sophie will say when you see her? Do you have a story ready?"

Hank's probing question halted Zach's troubled thoughts. "No story. Only the truth."

"She's going to be fuming. You know that?"

"She has a right to be."

"I wasn't sure if I should tell you this or not, but Sophie has been meeting with Blake Prescott."

Zach looked at his friend. "How do you know that? What were they talking about?"

"Don't know. Paula has heard her on the phone with him talking about the kids. I can only think of one reason she'd be talking to an attorney."

"Me, too." Custody. After his shady behavior today, she'd have every right to ask for guardianship of the kids. He knew in his heart that Sophie would be a far better guardian than he could ever be.

He touched the thick bandage over his eye. His flying career could be over and he might be facing a future alone. He rubbed his chin. The more he thought things through, the more confused he became. The various scenarios played out, each with a different and disastrous resolution. He needed help sorting it out.

A landmark sign flashed by. "Stop. Hank, pull over."

The car slowed. "Here? At the bridge?"

Zach exited the car the moment it stopped. Hank called after him.

"Watch your step. You only have one eye working right now. Your depth perception is poor."

Zach waved off his concern. He made his way along the overgrown path, taking care to watch his step. Daylight was fading and the bridge arched over the water in shadows, offering him the privacy and solitude he craved.

He'd come to this place several times since the death of his brother. He'd found a measure of comfort but he'd never needed it as much as he did right now.

Zach walked to the middle of the bridge and bowed his head, thankful that the Lord knew what he wanted to say because he could find no words. His life was so tangled he had no idea which wire to pull to begin unraveling it. His vision, letting Sophie down, loving Sophie, keeping his kids, were all one big Rubik's Cube of confusion.

He raised his head and looked around, but with one eye covered, he was handicapped as to what he could see. He trained his eye on one spot to stop the faint dizziness. His hands clutched the handrail, the feel of the aged wood reminding him of the work he'd done on the store and teaching DJ carpentry. With the exception of his first solo flight, nothing had given Zach as much satisfaction as teaching his nephew the family trade.

Zach stared at the wood rail in his hands. The aged cypress was smooth and warm and gracefully carved and it had been here standing strong for over a hundred and sixty years.

He let out a soft chuckle. "Thank you, Father." The solution to everything was suddenly clear. He knew what he would do and he might never have realized it with both eyes clear. It had taken a narrower focus for him to see what had been before him all the time.

One other thing was crystal clear: his deep love for Sophie. For the first time in his life, he understood what commitment meant and he wanted it—totally. Sophie and his kids, if it wasn't too late. He'd messed up royally. But he had his priorities in order now. His kids would always be first but Sophie was equally as important. If he had a chance with her.

The only way to start cleaning up his mess was to face Sophie and pray she would hear him out and understand and accept his apology. He didn't care how big a bowl of crow he had to swallow as long as she forgave him. He wanted her love but he'd settle for her friendship. Even though it would leave a hole in his heart for the rest of his life.

The grand opening for Maddie's Closet had ended over an hour ago. Sophie finished cleaning up, secured the facility and should be on her way home. But tonight the closet felt like a safe haven. The silence gave her the opportunity to think about her sister and reflect on the dream she had begun and had now been completed.

It also gave Sophie a place to hide. She wasn't ready to face anyone yet. Try as she might, her hurt over Zach missing the opening still stung. All the sensible reasoning she'd been through, all the logic and understanding she'd grasped didn't ease her broken heart, and no amount of self-scolding made it go away.

But she couldn't hide here forever. Walking into her office, she leaned over her desk and reached for her purse.

"Sophie."

Her heart froze. Zach.

All her rationalizing vanished as a surge of anger took over. The nerve of the man to show up here now. "I don't have anything to say to you." She spun around, preparing to unleash her fury, but stopped when she saw the large bandage over his left eye.

Her anger quickly dissolved into concern. "Oh, Zach. What happened? Are you all right?"

He came toward her and she moved to touch his face but he pulled away. She lowered her hand, searching his face for an explanation.

"I had eye surgery today. They fixed a problem with my retina."

The sense of being shut out washed through her. "What? Why didn't you tell me?"

He shrugged. "I didn't want anyone to worry. I remember how upset the kids were when I was late that night. I thought I'd take care of it myself."

"Did you injure your eye in the crash?"

"No, but the doctor discovered the problem on my follow-up visit. He sent me to a specialist in Jackson. Hank took me this morning for the surgery."

"How serious is it? Will you be able to see? Can you still fly?" Being a pilot was a big part of his identity. She knew losing the ability to fly a plane would be devastating for him.

"I don't know yet. The doctor is confident my eyesight will be fine, but we won't know for certain until the bandage comes off."

"Oh no. Zach, I'm so sorry." She grabbed his hand and squeezed. This time he didn't pull away. "I'll pray that you make a full recovery."

"Thank you. I'm sure it'll be fine." He held her hand firmly in his.

Their eyes locked and Sophie saw sadness and regret reflected in his gaze. She searched for something to say but Zach spoke first, finally releasing her hand, the cool air chasing away the warmth of his touch.

"How did the grand opening go?"

Not the topic she wished to discuss. She put on a confident smile. "Wonderfully. We had a big turnout and dozens of people offered their help. I wish you could have been here. Everyone asked about you." She crossed her arms. "I was so angry that you weren't here. You should have told me about the surgery."

He shrugged and glanced away. "It just seemed easier. Shutting people out is a habit."

Sophie set her jaw. The man was infuriating. "Easier for you, not us. You don't have to keep things from me or the children, Zach. It only makes it worse when you won't talk about it. You don't have to go through everything alone. That's what family is for."

He frowned. "I'm not good at talking about my feelings."

"This isn't about your feelings, this is about your life. You have people who love you and who want to support you and stand by you when you're dealing with things. We can't do that if you shut us out all the time. At the very least we could have been praying for you or come with you and rescheduled the opening."

"That's exactly what I *didn't* want. You've worked too hard to change things up for me."

Why didn't he understand? "*You're* more important than this closet." She sighed, tamping down her irritation. "When will you know about your vision?"

"I go back to Jackson tomorrow for the follow-up."

She moved away. "I wish I could go with you but I won't be here. I'll be leaving tomorrow."

"What? No, you can't. Not until I've told you…" He stopped and ran a hand through his hair.

"Told me what?"

"Nothing."

Typical of Zach. Avoid talking at all costs. "I'll come back and visit as often as I can if you'll allow me."

A deep frown appeared on his forehead, calling attention to the thick bandage over his eye. It tugged at her heart and spiked her concern. She hated seeing him like this.

"What do you mean, *allow you*?" he said. "Of course you can visit. Why would you think otherwise?"

"Why would I think anything else?" She couldn't hide the hurt in her voice. "You've been reminding me often enough that my time here is short."

"No. I didn't mean to give you that idea. I just didn't want you to feel obligated to stay here."

"You mean you didn't want to share the children."

He took a step toward her. "No. I was afraid you might try to take them away. Sophie, I know I haven't been the best dad to the kids. I'm still learning but you have to believe I love them."

"I do believe. I never doubted that."

"Good. Because I thought we could work out an arrangement. I'll do whatever is best for the kids, even if that means giving them up."

"What are you talking about?"

"I know you've been talking to Blake Prescott about gaining custody of the kids and—"

"What? Who told you that?" The downside to small-town life was dealing with gossips and busybodies.

"Hank said Paula heard you talking to Blake about the kids."

Sophie nodded. "Yes, but not about custody of the children. I wanted to talk to him about setting up financial accounts for them. I'll have money from the sale of my aunt's shop and her home and I wanted to set it aside for them. I would never take the children from you, Zach. You're their anchor."

Zach was relieved to hear her say that, but not for long. He couldn't imagine a life without her in it. She couldn't leave yet. Not when he had so much to say.

"What will happen to Maddie's Closet if you leave?" he asked her.

"Not my problem. Besides, you've hired someone to take over. Though I've never met her or had a chance to train her."

Zach winced at the sharp tone in her voice. Another strike against him. "She didn't accept the job."

Sophie turned away. "I'm sure you'll find someone."

"You could stay and run it, couldn't you?"

She tilted her chin upward and his heart sank. He knew that gesture and it meant she'd made up her mind and there was probably no changing it.

"No. I think I'll travel. Take one of those river cruises in Europe and see all the castles and old towns." She picked up her purse and moved past him.

He watched her walk away but couldn't let her leave. "Don't go." Slowly he walked toward her.

"Why not? There's no reason for me to stay here anymore."

"I can think of three."

She shook her head "The children will be fine with you. You'll find a job flying and it'll all work out."

"Actually, I have a new plan for the future. I'm going to take over Dean's contracting business. It'll provide steady employment and allow me to be home each night. Buck has hinted that he'd be glad to come back to work with me."

"But you said you hated the domestic life."

"That's before I had kids. I realized that if I had to choose between flying and taking care of the kids, I'd choose them every time."

"That's not what you said to me when I arrived."

"I know. I was scared you'd see what a lousy father I was and take the kids away."

"I told you I'd never do that."

He waved off her comment and moved closer. "I know. It was an idea that Hank threw out before he even met you. That whole thing with Maddie not telling us about her family, then you showing up suddenly, it was suspicious." He stepped closer. "Sophie, I've made so many mistakes. I've messed up with the kids and broken promises to them and to you. I never wanted to do that. You were right about how to deal with the kids' grief and about finishing this closet. It helped the kids and it helped me, too."

"I'm glad. Those kids mean the world to me."

"Me, too. Sophie, I hope someday you can forgive me for not being here today. The surgery ran late." He had no reason to think she'd understand, let alone forgive.

"I should apologize to you. I think I've placed too much emphasis on keeping promises. A friend suggested I was using it to keep from giving my heart away.

I think she might have been right. Things happen and sometimes promises get broken." She lifted her hand toward his face and gently touched his cheek. "Like delayed surgeries."

His chest filled with hope. "Does that mean you'll think about staying in Blessing?"

"Why should I stay?"

He took her hand in his and pulled her closer. "Because the kids need you. Everything got better when you arrived. You drew us together and made everyone feel safe and full of hope. The children are thriving now thanks to you."

Her fingers fluttered in his. "Is that the only reason I should stay? To make the children happy?"

It was now or never. He cleared his throat and looked into her hazel eyes. This was the time for truth. Time to trust that he was on the right path. "No. To make us all happy. To make *me* happy."

"Why?"

Her voice was so soft he wasn't sure he heard her. He brushed a strand of hair from her cheek. "I thought if you stayed, we could raise the kids together."

She tugged her hands from his grasp, catching him off guard. "How would that work, Zach? We become co-guardians? Run every decision past the other and decide what's best?"

He was handling this all wrong. "No. I wasn't thinking guardianship, exactly."

"What exactly?"

All he ever wanted was standing right in front of him but he was afraid he didn't have the courage to reach out and take it. He was standing at the edge of the cliff and there was no turning back. He had to say the words now or lose everything.

He took her in his arms, looking into her eyes praying for courage. "I love you. I have since you knocked on our door that first day. I was just too blind and closed off to see it. You belong with us. With me. I know I'm not the best husband material or father either but I can learn. I want to be that for you and the kids. I know I've done little to earn your love in return. I've lied, I've hidden things from you, I've shut you out, but I don't want to do that anymore. I want to be a real family but I only want to do that if you're there beside me."

A warm smile lit her face. She rested one hand on his cheek. "What took you so long? I've been in love with you from the moment I saw you with the children. You are the kindest, most gentle and devoted man I've ever met. And you're wrong. You're a great father. You're loving, supportive and firm, and I know you'll make a great husband, too."

"So you'll stay?"

"That depends on the terms."

"Terms?" Did she want a contract or some kind of agreement?

"What would my position be?"

The sparkle in her eyes fueled his hope. She was teasing. He slipped his arms around her waist. "I was thinking of a partnership."

The light in her eyes faded a bit. "A partnership?"

"A legally binding one. Lifelong in duration."

"Are you asking me to marry you?"

"I am." He inhaled the sweet scent that had captivated him from the first moment.

"Are you sure you can deal with a life without adventure?"

"Being a parent to three kids is all the adventure I need, but only if you're a part of it. Loving you will be a challenge, too, I think."

She laughed and slipped her arms around his neck. "That goes for you, too, Zach."

"Is that a yes?"

"Oh yes, yes."

Zach tilted his head and finally claimed the kiss he had been longing for. Holding Sophie in his arms filled the emptiness inside him that kept him from a full life. She was his other half. The missing piece to his heart.

Epilogue

Sophie held tight to Zach's hand in the family room a short time later. Zach had called a family meeting to explain about his surgery and reassure the children he would be okay. He'd also told them about taking over their dad's business.

DJ was particularly enthused about that. The girls were happy he'd be home more. But it was the announcement about their relationship that was most important. Zach and Sophie wanted to get their approval before making any more decisions.

Her heart swelled with love for Zach and spilled over to the children. She'd prayed for a solution that would be best for the children. She'd never expected it to turn out like this.

Zach glanced at her, squeezed her hand and took a deep breath. "There's one more thing." The children all looked at him with curious expressions. "Your Aunt Sophie and I wanted to talk to you about our family and the future." He squeezed her hand again.

He was as nervous as she was. She prayed the children would be happy with their decision.

DJ leaned forward, taking note of their clasped hands. "Are you two a thing?"

Sophie exchanged glances with Zach. Were their affections so obvious?

"If you mean are we together, then yes. We want to become your parents."

Katie tilted he head. "You mean like a new mom and dad?"

Sophie shook her head. "No one could replace your mommy and daddy. But we'd be your new family and we'd raise you just like your parents would have wanted."

Linney climbed up beside Sophie. "It'll be like having them back, kinda." She rested her head on Sophie's shoulder. "But I'll still miss my real mom and dad."

"Of course you will. We all will."

"So, does this mean you're getting married?" DJ asked, sounding puzzled.

Zach met her gaze and the love in his dark eyes sent a thrill through her veins.

Zach squeezed her hand. "Yes. We are. If it's okay with you?"

The children exchanged glances, then quickly nodded.

DJ grinned. "That's cool."

Katie joined them on the sofa. "Can we come to the wedding?"

Sophie smiled. "Of course. You can be my maid of honor."

"What can I be?"

Sophie kissed Linney. "The flower girl."

"What about DJ?" Linney asked.

Zach patted his nephew's knee. "I'll be needing a best man."

Linney grew serious. "Will we be a family forever?"

"Yes. We'll be here with you always."

"Promise?"

"Promise."

* * * * *

*If you loved this tale of sweet romance,
pick up other books
from author Lorraine Beatty.*

Her Fresh-Start Family
Their Family Legacy
Their Family Blessing

*Available now from Love Inspired!
Find more great reads at www.LoveInspired.com*

Dear Reader,

Welcome to Blessing, Mississippi, the setting of my next series. I hope you enjoyed your first visit as much as I've enjoyed writing Zach and Sophie's story.

Zach and Sophie both want families of their own. Sophie longs for the family she can't have, and Zach struggles to adjust from being a single guy to guardian of three children, and his fear that he will fail as a parent.

Sophie has had more broken promises in her life than most and as a result, she placed an unhealthy importance on keeping them. Her unrealistic expectations kept her from forming lasting relationships and being able to forgive others, especially her sister.

Forgiveness is one of the hardest instructions we're given as Christians. When we've been hurt or betrayed, it's painful to think of forgiving that person. We feel if we forgive those who have wronged us, we're saying it's okay. However, forgiveness isn't truly for them, it's for us. It frees us from the toxic burden of anger and resentment so we can move forward with our lives.

Zach and Sophie both must learn to see beyond past actions and events to find their way. Working together to create Sophie's sister's dream charity, and caring for their nieces and nephew, helps them come to terms with their emotions and their fears.

I love to hear from readers, so feel free to contact me at my website, lorrainebeatty.com, or like my author page on Facebook, Lorraine Beatty Author, or follow me @Lorraine_Beatty on Twitter.

Lorraine

COMING NEXT MONTH FROM
Love Inspired Suspense

Available September 1, 2020

SCENE OF THE CRIME
True Blue K-9 Unit: Brooklyn • by Sharon Dunn

Someone doesn't want forensic specialist Darcy Fields to live to testify in court. And now her case is being muddied by a possible copycat killer. Can Officer Jackson Davison and his K-9 partner keep her alive long enough to uncover who wants her silenced?

COVERT COVER-UP
Mount Shasta Secrets • by Elizabeth Goddard

Private investigator Katelyn Bradley doesn't expect to find anything amiss when she checks on a neighbor after a lurker is spotted near his house—until she foils a burglary. Now she and single father Beck Goodwin are in someone's crosshairs...and discovering what the intruder was after is the only way to survive.

FUGITIVE CHASE
Rock Solid Bounty Hunters • by Jenna Night

After her cousin's abusive ex-boyfriend jumps bail and threatens Ramona Miller's life for breaking them up, she's determined to help the police catch him—if he doesn't kill her first. Bounty hunter Harry Orlansky's on the job when he saves Ramona from his mark. But can they bring the man to justice?

FORGOTTEN SECRETS
by Karen Kirst

Left with amnesia after he was attacked and the woman with him abducted, Gray Michaelson has no clue why he's in North Carolina. But working with US marine sergeant Cat Baker, who witnessed the abduction, he plans to find the truth...especially since the kidnappers have switched their focus to Cat.

EVERGLADES ESCAPE
by Kathleen Tailer

US marshal Whitney Johnson's vacation is interrupted when drug dealers take over her wildlife tour boat and she overhears information that could destroy their operation. Evading capture by diving into the water, she washes up on Theo Roberts's land. Now if they want to live, Whitney and Theo must get out of the Everglades.

TREACHEROUS MOUNTAIN INVESTIGATION
by Stephanie M. Gammon

Years ago, Elizabeth Hart took down a human trafficking ring with a single blog post—and now someone's looking for revenge. But her ex-fiancé, Officer Riggen Price, won't let anyone hurt her...or the son he never knew he had. Can they face down her past for a second chance at a future together?

LISCNM0820

SPECIAL EXCERPT FROM

LOVE INSPIRED
INSPIRATIONAL ROMANCE

*When a television reporter must go into hiding,
she finds a haven deep in Amish country.
Could she fall in love with the simple life—
and a certain Amish man?*

Read on for a sneak preview of
The Amish Newcomer *by Patrice Lewis.*

"Isaac, we have a visitor. This is Leah Porte. She's an *Englischer* friend of ours, staying with us a few months. Leah, this is Isaac Sommer."

For a moment Isaac was struck dumb by the newcomer. With her dark hair tamed back under a *kapp*, and her chocolate eyes, he barely noticed the ugly red scar bisecting her right cheek.

Leah stepped forward. "How do you do?"

"Fine, *danke*. Where do you come from?"

"California."

"Please, sit. Both of you." Edith Byler gestured toward the table.

Isaac found himself opposite Leah and gazed at her as the family gathered around the table. When all heads bowed in silence, he found himself praying he could get to know the visitor better.

At once, chatter broke out as the family reached for food.

"We hope you'll have a pleasant stay with us." Ivan Byler scooped corn onto his plate .

"I…I'm not familiar with your day-to-day life." The woman toyed with her fork. "I don't want to be seen as a freeloader."

"What is it you did before you came here?" Ivan asked.

"I was a television journalist," she replied. Isaac saw her touch her wounded cheek and glance toward him. "But after my…my car accident, I couldn't do my job anymore."

Journalist! What kind of God-sent coincidence was that? He smiled. "Maybe I should have you write some articles for my magazine."

"Magazine?"

Edith explained, "Isaac started a magazine for Plain people. He uses a computer to create it. The bishop gave him permission."

"An Amish man using a computer?"

"Many *Englischers* have misconceptions of how much technology the *Leit* allows," Ivan intervened. "You won't find computers in our homes, or cell phones. But while we try to live not *of* the world, we still live *in* the world, and sometimes technology is needed to keep our businesses running. So, some bishops have decided a little technology is allowed."

"What's the magazine about?" Leah asked.

"Whatever appeals to Plain people. Farming. Businesses. Land management."

"And you want *me* to write for it?" she asked. "I don't know anything about those topics."

"But that's what a journalist does, ain't so? Learn about new topics," Isaac replied. Her opposition made him more determined. "Besides, you're about to get a crash course while you stay here. Maybe you'll learn something."

"I already said I had no intention of being a freeloader."

He nodded. "*Gut.* Then prove it. You can write me an article about what you learn."

"Sure," she snapped. "How hard could it be?"

He grinned. "You'll find out soon enough."

Don't miss
The Amish Newcomer *by Patrice Lewis,*
available September 2020 wherever
Love Inspired books and ebooks are sold.

LoveInspired.com

Get 4 FREE REWARDS!

We'll send you 2 FREE Books plus 2 FREE Mystery Gifts.

Love Inspired books feature uplifting stories where faith helps guide you through life's challenges and discover the promise of a new beginning.

FREE Value Over **$20**

YES! Please send me 2 FREE Love Inspired Romance novels and my 2 FREE mystery gifts (gifts are worth about $10 retail). After receiving them, if I don't wish to receive any more books, I can return the shipping statement marked "cancel." If I don't cancel, I will receive 6 brand-new novels every month and be billed just $5.24 each for the regular-print edition or $5.99 each for the larger-print edition in the U.S., or $5.74 each for the regular-print edition or $6.24 each for the larger-print edition in Canada. That's a savings of at least 13% off the cover price. It's quite a bargain! Shipping and handling is just 50¢ per book in the U.S. and $1.25 per book in Canada.* I understand that accepting the 2 free books and gifts places me under no obligation to buy anything. I can always return a shipment and cancel at any time. The free books and gifts are mine to keep no matter what I decide.

Choose one: ☐ **Love Inspired Romance Regular-Print** (105/305 IDN GNWC)   ☐ **Love Inspired Romance Larger-Print** (122/322 IDN GNWC)

Name (please print)

Address   Apt. #

City   State/Province   Zip/Postal Code

Email: Please check this box ☐ if you would like to receive newsletters and promotional emails from Harlequin Enterprises ULC and its affiliates. You can unsubscribe anytime.

Mail to the **Reader Service:**
IN U.S.A.: P.O. Box 1341, Buffalo, NY 14240-8531
IN CANADA: P.O. Box 603, Fort Erie, Ontario L2A 5X3

Want to try 2 free books from another series! Call 1-800-873-8635 or visit www.ReaderService.com.

---

*Terms and prices subject to change without notice. Prices do not include sales taxes, which will be charged (if applicable) based on your state or country of residence. Canadian residents will be charged applicable taxes. Offer not valid in Quebec. This offer is limited to one order per household. Books received may not be as shown. Not valid for current subscribers to Love Inspired Romance books. All orders subject to approval. Credit or debit balances in a customer's account(s) may be offset by any other outstanding balance owed by or to the customer. Please allow 4 to 6 weeks for delivery. Offer available while quantities last.

Your Privacy—Your information is being collected by Harlequin Enterprises ULC, operating as Reader Service. For a complete summary of the information we collect, how we use this information and to whom it is disclosed, please visit our privacy notice located at corporate.harlequin.com/privacy-notice. From time to time we may also exchange your personal information with reputable third parties. If you wish to opt out of this sharing of your personal information, please visit readerservice.com/consumerchoice or call 1-800-873-8635. **Notice to California Residents**—Under California law, you have specific rights to control and access your data. For more information on these rights and how to exercise them, visit corporate.harlequin.com/california-privacy.

LI20R2

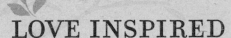

LOVE INSPIRED
INSPIRATIONAL ROMANCE

UPLIFTING STORIES OF FAITH, FORGIVENESS AND HOPE.

Join our social communities to connect with other readers who share your love!

Sign up for the Love Inspired newsletter at **LoveInspired.com** to be the first to find out about upcoming titles, special promotions and exclusive content.

CONNECT WITH US AT:

f Facebook.com/LoveInspiredBooks

🐦 Twitter.com/LoveInspiredBks

Facebook.com/groups/HarlequinConnection